To study, to learn, to safeguard that which is holy —and above all, to dare: that is the way of a Navigator.

Emeric of Rhada,
Grand Master of Navigators,
Early Second Stellar Empire period

Unhallowed knowledge brought the Dark Time, and fire from the sky, and death to men in ten times a thousand dreadful ways. So I say this to you: Seek not to know, for to know is to sin. Ask not *how,* nor *how much,* nor *how many. He who disturbs the mysterious ways of the Universe is heretic, an enemy of God and Man.* And he will burn.

Talvas Hu Chien,
Grand Inquisitor of Navigators,
Interregnal period

Ace Science Fiction books by Robert Cham Gilman

THE WARLOCK OF RHADA
THE REBEL OF RHADA
THE NAVIGATOR OF RHADA
THE STARKAHN OF RHADA *(coming in June 1986)*

ROBERT CHAM GILMAN
THE NAVIGATOR OF RHADA

ACE SCIENCE FICTION BOOKS
NEW YORK

This Ace Science Fiction Book
contains the complete text of
the original hardcover edition. It has been
completely reset in a typeface
designed for easy reading, and
was printed from new film.

THE NAVIGATOR OF RHADA

An Ace Science Fiction Book / published by arrangement with
the author

PRINTING HISTORY
Harcourt, Brace & World edition published 1969
Ace Science Fiction edition / March 1986

All rights reserved.
Copyright © 1969 by Robert Cham Gilman.
Cover art by Kevin Eugene Johnson.
This book may not be reproduced in whole or in part,
by mimeograph or any other means, without permission.
For information address: The Berkley Publishing Group,
200 Madison Avenue, New York, New York 10016.

ISBN: 0-441-56575-1

Ace Science Fiction Books are published by
The Berkley Publishing Group,
200 Madison Avenue, New York, New York 10016.
PRINTED IN THE UNITED STATES OF AMERICA

For The Spook, with love

Chapter One

In the last years of the Vykan Dynasty, Torquas the Poet reigned at Nyor. Power was divided among the Imperium, the star kings, and the Order Militant. The Second Stellar Empire stood at a crossroad of history. The forces of enlightenment, home rule, and stirring democracy faced the power of a great general. The danger was interstellar nuclear war. In the idiom of the age it was said that "sin has returned to test us." To the men of Vykan times the greatest sin was science.
—Varus Milenis, *The New Renaissance*,
late Second Stellar Empire period

To study, to learn, to safeguard that which is holy—and above all, to dare: that is the way of a Navigator.
—Attributed to Emeric of Rhada,
Grand Master of Navigators,
early Second Stellar Empire period

For many hours Kynan the Navigator had ridden the mare along the sea-cliff trail, and the animal, a hack rented in Gonlanburg, was tired, cross, and complaining. The rain that fell steadily from the darkly overcast sky sluiced off Kynan's skullcap and turned his clericals into a sodden ruin. He was thinking now that he should have hired an electric and chanced the batteries lasting the fifty kilometers to Melissande.

But it was too late now. The mare's clawed pads slipped and trembled on the rocky track, and from time to time she would turn her head to regard her rider reproachfully and ask, "Rest now, rider?"

Kynan, like all Rhads, had a great affection and sympathy for animals, and it sorrowed him to work the old hack so hard, but he could still hear the sounds of pursuit, so he had no option but to tell the mare that she could rest when they reached Melissande and urge her to greater speed.

The path had begun to rise into the basalt palisades of the Stoneland Peninsula. The Navigator had not traveled this track for many years, but he knew the way. As a child he had played here on the cliffs, stealing gulls' eggs and fishing in the surf of the Gonlan Sea. That was fifteen years ago: before Kreon sent him off to the Theocracy.

The mare stumbled and would have fallen, but Kynan's old skill on horseback returned, and he caught her head and guided her toward the center of the track.

He turned to look behind him, and he could see the two riders trailing him, cantering across a hard strand of beach below. They were warmen, Rhad by their harness, armed with electric flails and short lances.

There were still robbers in these parts, though why they should follow a Navigator was a mystery. Members of the Order were supposedly sacrosanct everywhere in the Empire; no Navigator carried anything of value but his microtapes and weapon. And for a layman to be caught with a Navigator's pistol in his possession meant instant arrest by the civil authorities of any world, no matter how backward.

What seemed most likely was that the two were AbasNavs, followers of the anticlerical party: professional killers of priests.

Ordinarily, no anticlericals would dare trespass on the personal land holding of the devout Kreon of Gonlan. But times, apparently, had changed.

What would Melissande be without Kreon? King of the Gonlani-Rhad, Kreon ruled all of Gonlan from the sea to the Arl Mountains and commanded a levy of twenty thousand warmen in the forces of the Rhadan Palatinate. Yet for all his power, the warleader was a good man—kind to Kynan, in any case. What other noble would make himself bond-father to a homeless warman's orphan and send him off-world to learn the way of a Navigator and consecrated First Pilot? Kreon had done that. And each year, at selection time, and on Kynan's saint-day, there had been a pouch with offering money and a letter. Kynan had them all, those letters. During the hard first years of his novitiate, and later, serving on starships parsecs from home, Kreon's messages reminded him that he was a Rhad and bond-son of a warleader.

Now they said that Kreon of Melissande was dying. If it was true, it would be a sad homecoming.

He wished that he could get more speed from the mare, but she was doing her best—and said so, grumbling breathlessly. Kynan found himself comparing Gonlan unfavorably with the other planets he had known. It was disloyal, but his urgency forced the comparison. On Gonlan there were no coal or petroleum deposits at all. The forests were too young. The only power source was the hundreds of leaping mountain rivers and the electric generating stations that dotted the single continent. There were electric hovercars in the towns, but for a long journey across the rugged hunting lands surrounding Melissande, only horses served—Rhadan horses, with clawed fighting feet and military bad temper.

Kynan once again turned his attention to the mounted men behind him. They had turned from the path to take another that led to the plateau, and for a moment Kynan thought that they might be abandoning the pursuit. There was no reason, after all, to assume that they were AbasNav partisans. They might simply be poachers. Then the Navigator realized that they were more sturdily mounted than he. If they chose, they could gallop across the plateau and cut him off from Melissande.

He wondered if he was overdramatizing his situation. A succession of Navigator superiors had told him that he was a young man with a highly developed imagination. He had done many a penance in the last fifteen years for a tendency to playact.

Still, the men *had* followed him from the spaceport, and it *was* a time of unrest. Navigators had been harassed by Imperial agents; some had even been arrested. Torquas XIII, the Galacton on far-off Earth, was said to fear that the Order of Navigators and grown too strong, too much a state within a state.

The beatified Emeric, of blessed memory, had foreseen that a time of conflict between the Empire and the Order might come. At the thought of the noble Rhad Grand Master, dead now these three hundred years, Kynan made the sign of the Star and murmured on Ave Stella. Though not yet canonized, Emeric of Rhada was regarded as a patron saint by all the Rhad.

Until the time of Marlana's rebellion in the first century of the Second Stellar Empire, the Rhad had been regarded as Rim barbarians. But with the marriage of Kier, the Rhad star king, to Ariane, the Regent and Princess Royal, the Rhadan Palatinate had increased in power and influence. And the Rhad clergy, the Navigators from the Ten Worlds, had lately been leaders in the fight for new freedoms.

Kynan, young and only just ordained First Pilot, was hardly worth a political murder on this lonely stretch of cliff. But he was a Rhad, bond-son of a warleader to Alberic, the present star king of Rhada. It would be best to take care.

The young cleric's hand sought the corded hilt of his pistol, and the solid reality of the weapon brought a grim comfort. This, at least, was simple and elemental. If one were attacked, one fought. And a fight meant either victory and survival or death and paradise. He had already fought on many worlds, in jungles where ancient colonies had reverted to savagery, in deserts where nomads had abandoned the old religion and set up new and blasphemous gods. It was all part of the way of the Navigator.

Like fragments of colored glass in a kaleidoscope, the events of the last weeks flashed through Kynan's mind. He saw again the saddened face of the novice who brought the superior's message into the control room of the Lyri starship Kynan had been commanding. "Kreon, your bond-father, is dying at Melissande—"

And Brother Evart, who like many young clerics, had an adolescent tendency to repeat rumors, had added, "It's said

Kreon was poisoned on Aurora—at the betrothal banquet of Karston and the Aurori heiress. Your bond-brother has been captured by the Aurori, and the Lady Janessa is hostage for him at Melissande."

Kynan thought of his proud adoptive brother Karston possibly in chains somewhere, and Janessa in the cells at Melissande. He remembered her only as a coltish green-eyed girl playing at soldiering in the stone rooms and corridors and among the trees in the gardens of Star Field, the Elector's residence on Aurora. But the memories were flawed with rumors of treachery and the betrayal of ancient friendships.

It all had an unreal and dreamlike quality to Kynan. Perhaps he had been cloistered too long, too far away from the political maneuverings of the Rim.

The mare raised her head and gave a warning. Ahead, in a narrow notch in the cliffs, she had seen the pursuers' mounts. She had been a war mare in her youth, and now she bared her teeth and said, "Rider, we fight—fight soon."

The animals knew before men when a fight was coming. They sensed their riders' intentions and emotions before men did themselves. Since the men of the First Empire colonized the Rhadan worlds, Rhad horses had been bred for war.

The Navigator decided not to run a gauntlet. The narrow shelving track suited him better than it would suit them as a battleground. It would at least force them to fight dismounted and give up the advantage of their fresh animals. He spoke gently to the mare to quiet her and dismounted. Then he took his pistol from under his arm and cleared the cumbersome mechanism that put the weapon into readiness. The short sword sheathed across his back he loosened in its leather case.

There was little else he could do in the way of preparing. If they really meant to fight him, they must come soon, for the light was going fast. To fight in darkness in this rain, on a ledge high above the sea, seemed a thing no outworld pair of warmen would do.

The mare nuzzled at him and nipped nervously with her sharp teeth. The hairs around her velvety nostrils were gray, but she was still trembling with the prospect of an engagement. "Fight," she breathed. "We fight."

"No," Kynan said. "Not you."

The animal's claws scraped the rocks. She was almost too tired to stand, but the anticipation of battle was upon her. "Fight," she said again.

"No," Kynan said sharply. "You go to Melissande. To the place above the sea. Tell them Kynan fights here—" He repeated his name carefully. "Kynan. Do you understand?"

"Ky-nan," the mare said.

"Go now." He turned her head back the way they had come and slapped her gently on the rump. The old animal stumbled away down the track toward the place where the high path crossed it. Once she paused and looked back, but Kynan said, "Go!" and she ambled off, head down and flanks heaving with weariness.

Moving purposefully, Kynan retreated to the very edge of the rock shelf. Underfoot, the mossy ground was slick with rain. A hundred meters below, white and frothing in the wet dusk, could be heard the long, rolling surf of Gonlan's northern sea. From this point of land to the ice barrier, two thousand kilometers to the north, no island or rock broke the surface of the dark ocean.

The wind was rising now, driving the cold rain like a lash and whipping the Navigator's cloak. He unclasped the sodden cloth and wound it about his forearm. Small protection against the flash of an electric flail—but if the highwaymen should ever come that near, all would be lost in any case.

Kynan thought of his bond-father at Melissande, and of his bond-brother, the proud one, a prisoner in some unknown keep. Even if the galactic spirit of the holy Star did not demand it, he promised he would fight to survive—and to avenge whatever offenses had been committed on Aurora against his family. He made the sign of the Star and recited the Prayer before Battle.

Then he drew his pistol, primed it, and waited.

Chapter Two

Unhallowed knowledge brought the Dark Time, and fire from the sky, and death to men in ten times a thousand dreadful ways. So I say this to you: Seek not to know, for to know is to sin. Ask not how, *nor* how much, *nor* how many. He who disturbs the mysterious ways of the Universe is heretic, an enemy of God and Man. *And he will burn.*
 —Talvas Hu Chien, Grand Inquisitor of Navigators,
  Interregnal period

I sought the knowledge of the atom. That I failed is my salvation. I recant all heresy and return in peace to the bosom of the Order.
 —Navigator Anselm Styr's confession
  on the scaffold at Biblios Brittanis, Mars,
  early Second Stellar Empire period

Three hundred years ago we burned researchers. Today we are on the verge of synthesizing plutonium. What might we not accomplish tomorrow—if there is peace?
 —Sal ben Yamasaki, Grand Master of Navigators to the
  Curia of Algol, middle Second Stellar Empire period

* * *

The starship in synchronous orbit above the surface of Gonlan was of ancient design. Like most of the other great interstellar craft in the known galaxy, it had been built more than ten thousand Galactic Standard Years earlier—in the time of the First Empire.

It was a huge vessel, as large as a small planetoid, and though only a dozen men were presently aboard her, she had been built to carry five full divisions of Imperial troops.

On her prow was emblazoned the spaceship and star of the First Empire, an insignia that the Theocracy of the Navigators had made their own. Within her kilometer-long hull, no man tended her powerful, eternal engines. Even the scientists of the Order had not yet solved the riddle of the power that had, for five millennia, driven this ship and a few thousand others back and forth across the galaxy at speeds that her present users were still unwilling to credit.

In the civilization of the Second Empire, the starships were the responsibility of the Order, and only the Order. Navigators trained in the Theocracy of Algol served every noble, every warleader in the galaxy—even the Galacton himself.

As late as a generation ago, the great starships had been lit within by torches, and their flight range had been limited by the slow fouling of the air within the hulls. But now the ancient life-support systems had been reactivated, the exterior scanning beams repaired. The holy Navigators, after three hundred centuries of study, retreat, inquisition, and devotions without end, were beginning to understand the miraculous machines bequeathed to them by the scientists of the Golden Age.

In the control room of the great ship, five cowled figures sat before the consoles. The bulkheads of the domed chamber were energized and transparent, so that the men and their machines seemed to float in open space against the cloud-girt disk of the planet below.

All wore the spaceship and star of the Theocracy. These were the Five: princes of the Order and controllers of the Navigators' galaxy-spanning intelligence apparatus.

The original Five had been assembled in the time of Torquas X (called the Heretic), the first Vykan Galacton to persecute the clergy. In times of danger to the Order, they commanded vast powers. Yet such was their knowledge that they, better than any men alive in this fourth century of the Second Stellar Empire, knew how many greater powers prowled the galaxy.

A tone sounded.

"Sensor beam locked on," the Technician reported.

Panels lighted before the five Navigators. Tiny three-dimensional figures moved along a path above a crashing surf. A tiny Rhadan mare shambled along a path to the sea.

"They've found him again," the Logician commented.

The Tactician said coldly, "If they take him, the game is over. Suggest we intervene."

"Negative," the Logician said sharply. "Our scanning area is limited. We can't tell who is in sight of that promontory. It could be anyone."

"Or no one," the Tactician grunted.

The Technician made an adjustment on his instruments, and the brightness of the tiny holographs increased. "We can't intervene without killing him—and blasting Gonlanburg and half the peninsula into gas."

"Suggest we consider just that," the Tactician said. "From the military point of view it would be justified. We still have the girl as a contact. We could activate the alternate plan."

The Theologian, least influential of the Five, said, "We are not justified in taking such action. May the God of Stars forgive you for even considering it."

The Tactician persisted. "We can't help him. Our weapons are too powerful and nonselective. And we cannot allow him to be taken. He is a nexus."

The Logician intervened. "If they had taken the girl, I would agree. That was what we foresaw when we had her implanted. But they didn't. She's in the cells at Melissande. A warhead would probably kill her, too."

The Tactician displayed a soldier's impatience. "The plan was always doubtful from the military point of view. We would do better to sterilize the area and begin again."

The last member of the group to speak was the Psychologist. Among his other duties was the coordination of the Five's activities. His voice was sonorous and persuasive. "The plan was never conceived as a military operation. Even the Order

Militant can't face the Empire on those terms—and it should not even try. You are too much the soldier, Tactician. Humanitarian considerations aside, a nuclear blast would bring the Imperials down on Gonlan and Rhada in force. We could never run the full course then. Not for another fifty years, perhaps more. The Galacton—"

"—is a fool," the Tactician said roughly.

"Precisely. We have waited three generations for this chance. In fifty years we may have another Glamiss Magnifico on the throne. We cannot risk too obvious a move now. Besides, I helped train the boy. He has powers he doesn't dream of. Let the plan operate."

"They are moving in on him," the Technician said.

"Pity the lad," the Theologian murmured. "Pray for him."

"You pray for him," the Tactician said grimly. "I'll just watch him die—and the plan with him—because people like you send men out armed with museum pieces." The irritation in his voice increased as he watched the tiny figure in his screen shielding his cumbersome flintlock weapon from the rain. "We could arm our people so that no one in the galaxy would dare touch them—and we pretend *that* is the best we can do."

"If the Empire suspected our energy weapons, the Theocracy would be a smoking ruin in a week," the Logician said sharply.

"And the Empire in a year," the Theologian added. "Shall we bring the Dark Time again?"

"I sometimes wonder if there ever really was a Dark Time," the Tactician grumbled.

The Psychologist laughed gently. "You are forgetting history, my military friend. It's time you went into Triad again."

The Tactician expelled his breath with a hissing sound. "Vulks make me sick."

"Vulks are children of the Star, too," the Theologian murmured with clerical unctuousness.

The Psychologist's mind touched for a moment the labyrinth of the Order's internal politics. The Theologian seemed more and more to tend toward the Stellar Heresy—that personification of God in the physical aspect of the stars. There were now priests who contended that the stars, in and of themselves, were holy. This verged on polytheism, and the gentle Yamasaki, current Grand Master of Navigators, had recently published an admonition on the subject.

The Psychologist sighed and considered how primitive still was the society of the Second Empire. That there could actually be controversy—even bloodshed—over so barbaric a dispute as the Stellar Heresy seemed grotesque in an age rediscovering atomic energy. Yet once, in the Dawn Age, men of the clergy had disputed over how many angels could dance on the head of a pin. Nothing really changed—

He returned his attention to the holograph before him. "What's happening now? I can't see him."

"He has gone under the rock outcrop," the Tactician said. "It will give him some cover while he reloads that antique firearm he's cursed with."

The Psychologist leaned forward for a clearer view of the tri-D display. In spite of all the training he had undergone to keep him objective and uninvolved during evolutions such as this one, he found that his heart was pumping sympathetically and there was a dryness in his throat.

The boy down there on the planet was a favorite of the Grand Master of the Order—though he would have been amazed to know it. The Psychologist had met him on a number of occasions and knew him to be a bright, dedicated, and almost painfully sincere priest of the Order.

For a moment the older man suffered a qualm of distaste for the way in which great movements used individuals. It was well enough to say that the good of the Order—the good of the Empire, for that matter—sometimes required great sacrifices of innocents. It was ever so in human history: before the Golden Age, before the Dark Time of the Interregnum, before, even, man had left his home planet to voyage among the stars.

But was it right, the Psychologist wondered as he had so many, many times before, to use men without their knowledge or consent? Did it matter that the boy preparing to fight for his life on that rain-swept coast below would gladly lay down his life for his faith, for the Order, and even for the Empire? Wasn't it a matter of morality rather than expediency? No, not expediency. That was too shallow a word for the needs of human destiny. One must live by certain great truths, the Psychologist told himself. For a priest of the Order of Navigators, the most shining of these truths was the absolute conviction that no temporal power could ever be allowed to interfere with the sacred freedoms of the Order. The five men in the starship control room believed it. The young Navigator on the sea cliff believed it. A million members of the Order spread across eight hundred thousand parsecs of space believed it.

That, *en fin*, was the heart of the dogma.

The Theologian (whom the others sometimes called the Preacher) subvocalized an Ave Stella for the young man thousands of kilometers below. The boy must reach Melissande before Kreon died. Only the old warleader could tell him who he was and what he must do.

The Preacher remembered Kynan's birth and the hopes it brought to the Order. He remembered, too, the spiriting away of the newborn, and the journey across the galaxy to Rhada and thence to Gonlan, to the holding of Kreon, devout and fierce true son of the faith.

The old priest raised his eyes from the holograph before him and looked into the night of space. The stars were thinly laid here on the edge of the known universe, but at the zenith he could see quite clearly the distinctive luminosity of the galactic lens.

He considered the forces at work in that spiral of stars and planets without number: the Empire, the Order, the uncommitted worlds where the Dark Time still lived. Currents of power sweeping across a mere two thousand worlds—and what else lived there on worlds where men had not ruled since the Golden Age?

We dare not fight among ourselves, he thought. *We men are too few, the powers of space too great.*

He looked again into the scanner screen. Doll-like figures moved against the gloom of a rain-washed sea.

Fight well, boy, the Preacher prayed. *Much depends on it.*

"Is this Veg Tran's doing?" The Tactician asked suddenly. "It has an AbasNav flavor."

"I doubt it," the Psychologist cautioned. "Tran can't know about the boy. The orders were probably given locally. But those thugs *are* anticlericals. They have that fanatic look."

"If not General Tran, then who?" the Preacher asked.

The Psychologist did not reply. It *was* possible that some petty power-seeker's urge to murder could shatter the plan— *the* plan that spanned the galaxy. *That,* he thought bitterly, *is the irony of history.*

Chapter Three

Though the way of the Navigator is peaceful, there will unfortunately always be those—unenlightened or irreligious—who may seek to interfere with him. A priest must avoid the use of force whenever possible, for we serve all mankind and concern ourselves with the saving of souls as well as the service of the holy vessels. Thus we are occasionally presented with a paradoxical choice: to submit to the ungodly or to do violence at the peril of our own souls. The beatified Emeric (of blessed memory) suggests the following: "If violence be unavoidable, the Navigator must seek to mitigate his sin of self-defense by fighting well. For it is well known that excellence in all things is the way of the Navigator and pleasing to God. After violence, however, a Navigator must seek a confessor and be assigned such penance as the confessor, in his wisdom, thinks suitable."
—From the *Handbook for Novices*,
Order of Navigators,
middle Second Stellar Empire period

Crouched under the rocky outcrop, a hundred meters above the sea, Kynan waited for his assailants.

There was no doubt in his mind about their intentions now.

He watched them close in, urging their nervous mounts down the slippery track. As they reached the inland edge of the narrow rock shelf, they seemed to realize that their quarry was alert to their intentions, ready and armed to fight for his life. This gave them pause. They knew of the explosive weapons of the Navigators.

Kynan watched them carefully. From his vantage point below them, he could see that they wore ordinary Rhadan harness, the working gear of the thousands of free-lance warmen to be found on the worlds of the Rhad. Each man carried a flail slung on his back and a dagger at his belt. They were not poor, for they both owned mailed shirts—new ones. In addition to flail and knife, each carried a short lance at his saddlebow.

They had dark, rather brutal faces. They were Gonlanborn: their stocky build proclaimed it. Gonlan was the most massive of the Rhad worlds. Their strong build might indicate that they were cyborgs and not men at all, but Kynan doubted it. Cyborgs were very rare on the Rim, almost unknown in the Rhadan Palatinate.

As Kynan continued to watch, the two men dismounted and spoke to one another in whispers. Kynan waited.

Presently, one called to him. "Come out, Navigator. We mean you no harm."

Kynan made no reply.

"I tell you there's nothing to worry about," the darker of the two said, ingenuously spreading his empty hands in the rain. "My sister is sick. She needs a priest. That's all."

Kynan cocked his pistol. The click of the mechanism was very clear in the dusk.

The warmen stepped behind their horses and conferred again. When Kynan saw them next, they had separated as much as the narrow track permitted, and one of them had unslung his lance and held it ready for a throw.

"Look, Nav," the other called, squinting into the half-light. "Come on out of there. There's nothing to be skittish about."

Kynan's legs ached with the effort of holding himself on the outcrop. He moved one foot to a more secure position. The man with the lance reacted swiftly. The missile arced through the rain to crash against the edge of the path, the steel point sparking. Kynan heard it, a moment later, clattering among the rocks far below.

There was another whispered talk between the two warmen, and one returned to where the horses stood waiting. He unslung the remaining lance and returned to stand with his companion.

The range was not more than twenty meters, and Kynan considered risking a shot. Still, the pistols were notoriously inaccurate at anything less than belly range and, once fired, took more than a minute to reload, prime, and cock. He decided to wait for better odds.

The man who had thrown his lance now unsheathed his electric flail. Kynan could hear the chains crackling and see the blue sparks through the curtain of falling rain.

The man with the lance raised his weapon and took careful aim. Kynan waited until his arm swept forward before straightening and moving sideways onto the rock ledge. At that instant, the assassin with the flail charged him. Kynan lifted his pistol and fired. The heavy bullet struck the man in the stomach, doubling him up and flinging him back against the cliff. He fell face down across his own flail, and there was a flash and the smell of scorched flesh as the weapon overloaded and burned out.

Kynan felt a stab of pain in his thigh and looked down to see that the thrown lance had pierced his leg just above the knee. He stumbled and fell, snapping the haft of the weapon, the ripped muscle drawing a moan of agony from him.

The second assassin was charging, flail held high. Kynan dropped his useless pistol and pulled his sword over his shoulder. He caught the first sweep of the flail on his blade, and a shower of sparks scattered over the rubber grip of the sword.

Kynan forced himself to his feet and leaned against the cliff as his assailant took a fighting stance with his back to the sea.

The man was breathing hard, and his face was distorted with anger. "All right, holy Joe. Now—now, we'll see!"

Kynan put his weight on his uninjured leg and thrust. He could not afford a long fight—he was losing too much blood for that. Even with the lance point in his thigh, he must attack or die.

The flail crackled by his face, trailing sparks. Kynan aimed a series of head cuts, feinted, swept his point down across the hand holding the flail.

The man screamed with pain and anger and changed weapon hands. He charged heedlessly and caught a ringing blow on his steel cap. A single chain brushed across Kynan's injured leg, and the electric shock almost knocked him down. He could feel the warm blood streaming, and he felt a growing weakness.

The light was going swiftly, and the rain made the footing dangerous. Kynan caught the assassin's cheek with his point and laid the dark face open to the bone.

The warman, more heavily built than the Navigator, closed with him hilt to hilt. Sparks showered as the chains touched the sword blade. Kynan looked into the dark eyes, the bloody face, and saw the look of the priest-hater. There were many such throughout the galaxy, men who hated the clergy for real or imagined wrongs. But they were rare on Gonlan, and Kynan wondered what had happened among the Rhad to conjure up this kind of dark passion.

"I'll kill you—Nav—kill you—" The man's voice was harsh, strangling in his throat.

Kynan could feel himself weakening. There was no time now for anything but survival. His free hand found his knife and drew it. The Navigator let the other force him back a step, then twisted toward the cliff's edge.

The man lost balance, and Kynan, with a short, desperate motion, drove the knife home.

The assassin dropped the flail, turned, and ran—his hands holding his stomach. He ran headlong into the rock wall, feeling nothing but his mortal wound, turned, ran again across the track and straight over the edge. He made no sound as the rain and night consumed him.

For what seemed to be a long time, Kynan stood on the ledge, his breath coming in deep, painful sobs. It was dark now, and the wind drove the rain in gusts before a rising storm.

Kynan's wounded leg gave way abruptly, and he found himself stretched out on the wet rocks of the path with the rain stinging his face.

He was very weak, and his whole side seemed on fire with

the pain of the lance head in his thigh. But he dragged himself toward the body of the assassin he had killed with his pistol.

Still stretched out at full length and with his strength all but gone, Kynan inspected the contents of the dead man's pouch by the tiny light of his electric torch.

There was nothing significant: only a half-dozen Imperial coins. The bearded image of Torquas, the Galacton, was etched familiarly into the stainless steel disks.

The lance head felt like a drop of molten metal in his thigh. He dropped the torch, and it went out. He fumbled for it among the wet rocks and could not find it.

He called out to the assassin's horses to come to him, but the beasts had wandered away up the path now that the fighting was done.

Kynan tried next to drag himself into the lee of the cliffs, for he had begun to shiver uncontrollably with cold and shock. In his confusion he crept in the wrong direction. He had reached the edge of the drop to the sea and was almost over the edge when he fainted.

Chapter Four

Fear the Vulk, for he sees without eyes and knows the black arts and dreams of the blood of children. He is not as men. He is without loyalty.
—Preface to *The Vulk Protocols,* authorship unknown, Interregnal period

—and it is my wish that my descendants honor this Patent while the House of Rhad rules in Rhada. The Vulk known to men as Gret has been my honored friend and my father's friend. My trust in him is complete and without condition. For howsoever long the Vulk Gret wishes to serve the House of Rhad, let him be known as Royal Vulk to this family. Given this thirtieth day of the seventh month of the year 6,001 Galactic Era: this sixtieth year of my reign as Kier, second star king of Rhada.

—Excerpt from a Patent of Nobility,
The Rhadan Archives,
early Second Stellar Empire period

The alien creature with the ancient title faced the councillors of the Gonlani-Rhad in the hall of Melissande. Like all of his kind, Gret was small in stature—not more than a meter and a half high—and delicately made. His overlarge head, quite hairless and pallid, gleamed in the torchlights. The angry warmen who faced him stood silent, watching the smoothly featureless face, the sensitive mouth, and the motionless, tapering hands resting on the carved bow of the lyre he carried.

The men of Gonlan: Crespus, the General; Kreon's warlock, Baltus; Tirzah, the Constable; and LaRoss, the First Minister, were hearing counsel from the Vulk—counsel they did not want to heed.

"There was no need for the star king to send you, Master Gret," General Crespus said, after a long silence. "This is a local matter. We can handle it ourselves."

Gret gave a very human sigh. For years beyond counting, he had lived among men. He had served the first star king of Rhada, and the star king Kier of blessed memory. He had counseled Kier's son and grandson and now his great-grandson, Alberic, who was growing old. In Gret's nonhuman mind lay the memories of millennia and a profound understanding of the savage and wondrous creatures called men.

Gret's fingers struck a vibrant note from the lyre. "The making of war on an allied nation-state is scarcely a local matter, General. The noble Rhad asks that you consider very carefully. The friendship between the Rhad and the Aurori is long standing, sanctioned by the Order and the Empire." Privately, Gret wondered about the Empire in this connection. But this was hardly the place to voice his doubts. Long ago, in Kier's time, the ties between the Empire and the Rhadan Palatinate were close. Gret remembered Ariane, sister of the first Torquas, who had married into the royal family of Rhada. The troubadours had sung of her:

> *Men called her Princess,*
> *Men called her Queen,*
> *Wore she armor of purest gold*
> *And loved she well her Rim-world king,*
> *She whom the warmen called—Ariane!*

But these were old memories of other times. The world was *now,* as one found it. With the threat of civil war on the Rim—

"You have already brought war very near," Gret said, "by stealing the heiress Janessa from Star Field. Alberic offers to mediate."

"Alberic is growing old," growled Tirzah. "Perhaps he forgets what it means to be a Rhad warman, but we have not, Master Gret."

Baltus, the warlock, said, more mildly, "Our king is dying, Gret. Poisoned on Aurora where he went in friendship. Our heir is captured. You know young Karston. He is not called the Proud for nothing. By now he may have been killed. I can't imagine anyone holding him alive for very long. So then, are we expected to do nothing?"

The Vulk inclined his head. "I admit your provocation has been great, and the men of Gonlan are honorable. The noble Rhad takes all this into consideration. But he asks that you think what war on the Rim will mean." The thin lips formed a sad smile. "I know better than most what civil strife brings. I remember the Dark Time. Long before any of you were born, I fled from world to world in peril of my life because I was a Vulk, and for my kind there is safety only in the rule of laws—laws that crumble in war. Five hundred years ago men fought with spears and swords and dropped stones from the starships. Now, thanks to science"—he nodded ironically to the warlock—"we have rediscovered gunpowder and the art of bombing cities. Are we to light the fuse here on the Rim? What are laws for, then? What is the purpose of the Empire and the nation-states if not to bring justice without war?"

General Crespus stared red-eyed at the Vulk. "The nation-state exists for the protection of its people and its honor. Perhaps you've been too long on the Inner Planets, where things are done differently. Here on the Rim we are not afraid of war."

"Spoken like a true general, Crespus," Gret murmured. "Yes, it's so I have served the Rhad at Nyor—the first Vulk to be an ambassador to the Imperial Court from a Rim world, thanks to Kier and Ariane. None of you would remember them, for it was long ago, before you were born. But they had a vision of a Second Stellar Empire greater than the first: a supernation of worlds at peace, governed by laws and just men. It has not yet come to pass—but it must, or the Dark

Time will come again. War is a cancer. It spreads swiftly. If Gonlan and Aurora begin to fight, all the Rhadan worlds will become involved. Loyalty to the Empire will disintegrate—because the Rhad are all like you. 'Blood and honor,' General. The clergy will take sides. Men of the Order will fight one another for their home worlds. It takes very little to start a war, gentlemen. It is very difficult to stop one. I ask that you consider carefully. Your star king, Alberic of Rhada, asks it—implores it, if you will. Return Janessa to Aurora."

"Never," Tirzah declared, his hand on his flail. "What will happen to Gonlan if our king can be poisoned and our prince kidnaped without fear of retaliation?"

Gret sighed. He felt suddenly old and weary. He wished sadly for the comforting mind-touch of Erit, his sister-wife. But she was far away, on Rhada. No, he would have to face this alone, knowing that he could not prevail against human pride and anger.

"The Order of Navigators maintains an enclave on Aurora," he said. "They are mining sacred ores there. What do you imagine they will do if you attack the planet?"

The cold, rain-laden wind from the sea swayed the tapestries hanging on the walls of the ancient hall. Gret shivered for a moment, thinking that he was, indeed, growing old at last because he stood here with these warmen talking of peace and battle, and yet a part of him yearned for the comforting warmth of his quarters in the star king's great house on Rhada. There was a time, he thought, when electric heat and soothing surroundings would have been the farthest things from his mind while engaged on such a mission as this.

Baltus, the warlock, rather more scientist than warman, was the only hope for a peaceful settlement here, Gret knew. He wondered if he had done a wise thing in invoking the threat of the Navigators, however. In times past, the Order had persecuted warlocks unmercifully for delving into the ancient mysteries and intruding into the priestly preserves of Golden Age knowledge. The persecutions were almost unknown now, but the memory of those desperate times during the Interregnum between the Empires was a heritage of all warlocks, some of whom were now members of the AbasNav party.

"The Order will behave the way the Order has always

behaved," Baltus said. "The Aurori Navigators will pilot the Aurori starships. The Navigators of Gonlan will pilot ours. The clergy cannot afford to take sides in a dispute such as this."

"The Navigators have already taken sides, Baltus," Gret said flatly. "Their enemy is the Empire. It hasn't always been so, nor will it always *be* so. But since Torquas X's time, there has been conflict between the Order and the government of the Empire."

"Well, then," Tirzah said brusquely, "what is that to us?"

"Only this. The Auroran enclave is important to the Order. So important, I fear, that it might cause them to abandon their traditional evenhandedness. If you attack Aurora, Rhada may come under an interdict."

"Impossible," Crespus declared. "The Ten Worlds of Rhada are devout and God-fearing. Excommunicate us? Impossible, I say. Why, more than likely the Navigators will favor us in any war with the Aurori. Firstly, because the treacherous attack on the betrothal feast was a betrayal of the laws of hospitality and a breach of the peace of God. And secondly, because the Aurori have attacked the bond-father and bond-brother of a holy Navigator. Kynan—you know the boy, Gret. Kreon's adoptive son."

"You have sent for him, of course."

"We have, naturally. Kreon insists on seeing him. Some of our people even consider him the heir to Gonlan, now that Karston may be dead," said LaRoss, speaking for the first time.

Gret turned his attention fully to the First Minister. Vulks did not "see" as humans did. Their perceptions were stimulated by mental energies and that universal principle that the ancient priest-kings of long-ago-destroyed Vulka called "the life force."

With great effort and human cooperation, the Vulk could enter the human mind. Even without a human's acquiescence, a mature Vulk could sense much that transpired within a man. But LaRoss, Kreon's First Minister, was that human rarity to Gret: a completely shielded personality. No inkling of what went on within the minister's tightly controlled brain reached the questing Vulk.

"Do you believe Karston dead, Minister?" Gret asked.

La Ross shrugged and wrapped his dark cloak around him against the chill air in the hall. "I can only tell you what I saw with my own eyes, Vulk. It would be well if you told it to Alberic just as I tell it to you. He is a Rhad and a warman, and he should understand what it means." He walked to the narrow window and stood for a moment studying the stony seacoast far below. Night was falling, and the long swells of the Gonlan Sea broke in bursts of dark silver on the rocky coast.

LaRoss spoke quietly. "It was a happy occasion, as you might imagine. Kreon and Karston went to Star Field as friends and allies. There was no need—or so we thought—for anything more than a ceremonial escort. After all, Karston and Janessa were promised when they were still children, and there has never been war between Aurora and Gonlan." He regarded the Royal Vulk of Rhada with narrowed eyes. "Between Aurora and *Rhada*, yes. Before Gonlan became part of the Rhadan Palatinate—in Aaron the Devil's time—the Rhad and the Aurori warred and raided. But I forget that you must remember that yourself. You were Aaron's councillor—"

The Vulk smiled thinly. "I was Aaron of Rhada's fool and minstrel, Minister. In those days, Vulks had no titles."

LaRoss gave a mock bow. "Forgive me. I forget that it was Kier who changed all that. The great king of the Rhad."

"He was," Gret said, "and well you know it. The very greatest of the Rhad. Greater even than the beatified Emeric. But go on."

"There's little enough to tell, actually. We arrived at Star Field, and the Elector greeted us well—" LaRoss grimaced. "I admit to being at least partially at fault in this. I have always favored the Auroran alliance for us. I thought the Elector an honorable man. I was wrong. First Kreon was taken ill at the feasting. Then we were attacked—without warning and without the hope of any real resistance. Karston was taken. Several of our officers were killed—"

"The men who attacked you—?"

"You wouldn't expect them to wear Auroran harness, would you, Master Gret? No, nothing of the sort. Their arms and armor were civilian design—they could have been from any one of the Ten Worlds. But they were *on* Aurora. They were *in* Star Field. Could they have done that if they were strangers?"

Gret made no reply.

LaRoss shrugged and turned away, renewing his scrutiny of the restless, darkening sea.

Tirzah said, "They reckoned without a full understanding of us, though. We are Rhad, after all"—he flushed momentarily and then continued—"men of Gonlan, in any case. We fought our way back to our ship—and we took Janessa with us. She is here now. Below, under guard. That is all there is to say except that Aurora will regret it."

Gret said, "You, General Crespus. Were you there?"

"No, by the holy Star. I wasn't, and I should have been. But I was here, inspecting the garrison."

"It's just as well," LaRoss said moodily. "If Crespus had been taken or killed, Gonlan would be without a military leader. I believe that was the intent of the operation. My agents on Aurora send word that they are mobilizing for war —invasion, if they can manage it."

Gret shrugged and caressed his lyre so that the strings hummed softly. "You have their heiress, after all."

Tirzah made an impatient gesture. "No, Master Gret, things have gone too far. It's war, and that's all there is to it. I'm sorry our Alberic is displeased, but nothing can be done. We ask only that he stay out of it and allow us to settle with the Aurori in our own way."

Alberic, Gret thought sadly, too old now to take the field against insurgent vassal states, too old to keep the peace on the Rim. Why was it that something warned him that this choice of time, place, and combatants was not coincidental? Was it the plaguing Vulk sense of history? That knowledge that came with long, long life and much knowledge of the galaxy's only star-voyaging race, man the predator?

One last throw, then, the Vulk thought, like the counter falling on a board where a lost game of stars and comets must be played to the end.

"War between Gonlan and Aurora will give the Imperials an excuse to intervene, councillors. You know that, of course. But do you know what it means? For two hundred years home rule has been a fact in the Rhadan Palatinate. What happens when Torquas's warships appear here 'to keep the peace'?"

"Torquas would not dare," General Crespus said positively.

The Vulk sighed. There was no convincing these touchy outworlders. Perhaps it was as Crespus had said—perhaps he *had* been too long among the politicians of the Inner Worlds and had forgotten that here, on the Rim, disputes were settled with blows and bloodshed. But intervention by the Imperials seemed a virtual certainty to Gret, who knew the temper of the Galacton's court. Home rule, democracy, these were despised concepts in the Imperial city of Nyor, half across the sky.

But surely there was something more in this? There was a missing factor somewhere, a piece of the puzzle gone, an element not yet clear. The Vulk's narrow shoulders sagged wearily. Somehow, he was failing in his duty. His intuition told him that he had not penetrated to the heart of the matter, yet he was at a loss how to continue. Perhaps it might be best to go to Kreon and ask to probe his mind. A desperate thing to do with, and to, a dying man. The strain could kill a human untrained in the mind-touch. And should a man die while sharing his mind with a Vulk, the symbiote shared his death. Yet there seemed no other way. Vulks had been dying for men— and at their hands—for thousands of years with a docility and loyalty few men understood. What would one more death mean to history, Gret wondered? To his own people, the loss would be grievous—there were so few Vulks left. But to man, to his Empire and his destiny—?

He turned his featureless face to LaRoss and was about to command the First Minister to take him to the dying star king's quarters when the ancient stones of Melissande began to throb to the slow beat of a huge, muffled drum. The men in the hall stood quite still, listening. Then through the rainfall came the mournful call of a military trumpet sounding last post.

Tirzah drew the sign of the Star on his mailed chest. His eyes were suddenly filled with tears. "Kreon is dead," he said.

Chapter Five

TORQUAS XIII *(called the Poet), Eighteenth Vykan Galacton of the Second Empire, 6,212 GE-6,252 GE. Son of Torquas XII and Mariana of Eleuthera (daughter of Silentus the Thin, Amir of Epsilon Cygnus 9). Last of the Torquans, Torquas XIII came to the throne after assassination of Torquas XII by officers of the Vegan Imperial Household Troops. He is known to historians primarily for his association with General the Honorable Alain Veg Tran, victor of the Battle of Eridanus (6,209 GE), Imperial Proconsul (6,215 GE-6,220 GE), and leader of the AbasNav (anticlerical) party from 6,210 GE to 6,220 GE. . . .*
  —Nav (Bishop) Julianus Mullerium,
   Anticlericalism in the Age of the Star Kings,
   middle Second Stellar Empire period

As the authors of almost every revolution that distracted the empire, the Praetorians will demand attention; . . . in their arms and institutions we cannot find any circumstances that discriminated them from the legions, save a more splendid appearance and a less rigid discipline.
  —Fragment found at Nyor (Tel-Manhat), Earth,
   attributed to Edward Gibbon, a historian of the
   middle Dawn Age period

* * *

Those who do not learn from history are doomed to repeat it.

Dawn Age proverb

In Earth's northern latitudes, the season was spring. From the terraces of Tran's hunting lodge atop the ridge of mountains in the Western Land, the fertile Saclara Valley could be seen through the haze—green from the mountains to the bay, dotted with orchards and thicket-like parks.

To the man from Gonlan, the land seemed lush, overly ripe, and tamed. Yet he knew that packs of great wild dogs roamed the fields of Saclara: dogs maintained by the general as game for the blood sports he loved to the exclusion of almost all else except war and politics.

The people of the valley, who were descendants of the original survivors of Earth's Dark Time, habitually went about Tran's lands in company with armed Vegans, members of the general's personal guard. This was said to be for their own protection against the wild, semi-intelligent dogs; but it seemed to Karston, born to the freedom of the Rim, that the Veg soldiers served as much to suppress any dissent among the tenants as to protect them from the packs.

From his vantage point on the uppermost terrace of the fortress-like lodge, Karston could see a party of Veg warmen riding up the long, straight path from the valley. There were six of them, and the scales of the armored horses glinted in the warm spring sunlight.

There were ground cars in the lodge: three of them. But these were reserved for the personal use of General Tran and his secretary, a stocky Vegan warlock named Quinto. The machines were the newest hovercar design from Nyor, and they could cover the distance from the lodge overlooking Saclara to the spaceport at St. Francis Town in less than an hour. But the tame look of the land was deceptive, and since it was impossible to travel by hovercar anywhere except on the floor of the valley or along the muddy shores of St. Francis Bay, most of the general's people were horsemen.

Karston studied the animals with interest as the war party approached the lodge's outer defenses. Vegan chargers were descendants of the original breeding stock taken to the Vegan planets by the Imperial officers of the First Empire. Like the horses of Rhada, they had been altered over countless generations to suit the requirements of the men who bred them. And whereas on the Rhadan worlds the animals had been mutated to produce mounts of great swiftness, ferocity, and intelligence, the Veg had bred a strain of armored beasts, immensely strong but sullen and devoid of the rudiments of language and telepathy. Karston watched the sunlight glistening from the armored carapaces and the articulated platelets of silvery hide. The animals suited the Vegan character, he thought with Rimworld arrogance. The Veg were specialists in defense and dedicated to victory through intransigence rather than maneuver.

But the troop had a certain elegance, Karston had to admit —a flamboyance of manner and dress that belied the true character of the races of Vega. The harness worn by the warmen was of extreme design, heavily ornamented with gems and precious metals. The officer in command wore a circlet of brilliantly colored feathers in his helmet, and the horsemen carried crossbows slung across their backs. Vegan Imperials— the praetorians of the Second Stellar Empire. All were laughing and talking, and there seemed no semblance of discipline or order in their approach. Karston wondered what this particular detachment had been doing below in the hazy valley. The officer carried a bundle, slung in a stained black cape, at his saddlebow.

"I see by your expression that you don't think much of Household Imperials."

Karston turned to the speaker. General the Honorable Alain Veg Tran had come onto the terrace quite soundlessly. Karston studied the square face, ornamented with a small beard around the tiny, compressed mouth. Tran's dark eyes were like lumps of tarnished silver in the sunlight. He was a large and athletic man, running slightly to fat now in his fortieth year. His hair was long and caught with silver clasps in the Vegan style, and he wore the unadorned tunic of a Vegan Imperial prefect. His near-austerity contrasted strangely with the peacock magnificence of the troops approaching the lodge gatehouse.

"They're well enough for parade troops, I suppose,"

Karston replied, with a touch of insolence.

A movement of Tran's thin lips suggested a smile. "Don't allow their manner to fool you, my young friend. In open battle—give me Rhadans every time, of course. But when the task is subtle, there are no better men than the warmen of the Vegan Imperials. I should think the operation on Aurora would have convinced you of that."

"Janessa is on Gonlan, not here, General. At least half the operation failed."

Tran leaned on the terrace rail and looked out over the valley. Far to the west, toward the Sierras, great white towers of cumulus clouds rose from the haze. "I think it is time you learned some facts, Karston. If you are going to dabble in interstellar politics, you must become a realist."

Karston frowned at the older man but said nothing. It occurred to him for the first time that his anxiety to come into his inheritance had brought him to a risky position. He was alone in an Imperial stronghold; in the power of a man whose reputation for ruthlessness was legend throughout the Empire. And he had—his mind would not accept the word "betrayed," but his actions would certainly be so regarded among his own people if they knew—he had *contrived* to align himself with powers operating on a scale far beyond his own limited hopes and expectations. Alain Veg Tran *was* the Imperial power. Torquas was a verse-writing, remote figurehead. Weak Galactons created strong generals. Tran and his AbasNav Party controlled the forces of the Empire: that much was fact.

At the outset, Karston had imagined he could use this power to take what would one day be his, in any case—the power in Gonlan. But power was tricky stuff to handle, and now the young prince was having some second thoughts. Pressure was useful, yes. But it was a matter of degree. And from the first day Karston had allowed the agents of General Tran to approach him on Gonlan without ordering them arrested and delivered to the star king for judgment, the possibility of his own plans being engulfed in the larger battle had existed. But his pride made it impossible for him to admit fear or doubt. Now he replied to General Tran with characteristic arrogance.

"You'll find no one more *realistic*, as you put it, than I anywhere in the galaxy, my dear general. I know what I'm doing."

"I have no doubt you think so," Tran said. "But I'm afraid I must begin to correct some of your more naive notions." He turned to regard the young man with those cold, silvery eyes. "When my agents reached you and offered to speed your father's incapacity so that you could rule on Gonlan, we expected nothing less than your agreement. All the Rhad are nothing if not greedy for power. Or am I being too severe on you outlanders? No matter. We've done our part, in any case. Though I must admit that I was a bit surprised at your willingness to have your father—ah, eliminated." The eyes grew even more metallic in the bright daylight. "But you were never close to Kreon, were you?"

Karston stared sullenly at the general. This interview wasn't going well. It wasn't bringing him any closer to his objective, which was to be returned now to Gonlan with an Imperial starship and troops for the war of annexation against Aurora.

"Kreon's favorite was always your bond-brother, I believe," Tran said.

Karston made an impatient gesture. "Kynan is lowborn. He does not figure in this."

Tran smiled and shook his head. "Karston the Proud. You're well named, my arrogant young friend. But listen—listen carefully. Kynan figures in all this far more than you realize. I am surprised you haven't been able to sort out the realities of the situation even yet."

"A priest—a Navigator. He's not even a real Rhad. My father adopted him."

"Exactly. And with you—ah, missing—who is now star king of Gonlan?"

Karston paled angrily. "Not Kynan. Never Kynan!"

"Who else but Kynan? The shock of what has happened will be wearing off soon among the Rhad at Melissande. Crespus is a blustery old fool off a battlefield, and Tirzah's as arrogant as you are. But the warlock Baltus and LaRoss are realists. It wouldn't be the first time in history that a Navigator became star king of an Imperial province."

"But *I* am the heir!" Karston said, in a strangled voice.

"No one knows whether or not you are alive, now, do they?"

"I must return to Gonlan at once, then!"

"Slowly, slowly. Everything in its proper place. You here. Kynan at Melissande—" Tran's smile grew icy. "And Janessa in the hands of your warlike outland relations." The smile faded, and the general's face seemed suddenly to be hewn from stone. "I must have war between Gonlan and Aurora. I must have rebellion in the Rhadan Palatinate. That's what all this has been about. You didn't imagine I've set all these forces in motion just to put you on a petty throne? You couldn't be so limited in your viewpoint, Karston, not really."

Karston frowned. His throat felt dry, and his heart had begun to flutter in his chest. "You never intended to take Janessa—"

"What possible good would she do me here? I wanted the Rhad of Gonlan to take her. Kidnaping. A breach of courtesy, of a marriage contract—and a long-standing peace. What could be better?"

"I don't understand," Karston protested.

General Tran sighed heavily and looked again at the quiet valley. "Each man plays out his part on the stage intended for him by fate, destiny—whatever you wish to call it, Karston. I was born a great prince. In truth, I should have become Galacton." He shrugged. "But it wasn't to be. I'm a Vegan. When Glamiss the Magnificent founded the Second Empire, a member of my clan stood at his side. When the last Pretender died after the Battle of Karma, an ancestor of mine held Glamiss of Vyka's sword." Tran indulged his thin smile again. "Perhaps if he had *used* it at that moment, history would have been different. Perhaps I would rule in Nyor now instead of Torquas—and Torquas could spend his life writing those silly poems he loves so. But it didn't happen that way—and I am the Prince's general, not the Prince. Still, with the Empire saddled with a Torquas—someone must actually *rule*. For twenty years, *I* have done that." He turned to face the young warman sternly. "But for each of those twenty years, I've been dogged and balked and harassed by the Navigators." His voice turned scornful and angry. "Our holy men. Because they control the starships, they imagine they are our moral preceptors. They've done much that's useful—I'd be the last to deny that. But their time is gone. Their age of faith is over. There is not room in the galaxy for *two* powers. It must be the Empire or the Order.

It can't be both. And your little war on the Rim is the fuse that lights the charge that destroys them at last." He began to pace the terrace restlessly. Below, the troop of Vegan warmen had reached the lodge gates. The officer commanding called out to the general, holding aloft the object that had hung at his saddlebow. Karston, though accustomed to violence and bloodshed, was shocked to see that it was a human head.

Tran raised his hand in acknowledgment. "Well done, Captain!" he called. He turned to regard Karston coolly. "A Navigator's head, young sir. Specifically, the head of the Navigator who flew the starship that brought you here from Aurora."

Karston gasped at the sacrilege and unconsciously made the sign of the Star.

"It had to be done," Tran said. "He knew it, too. That's why he took refuge with the Saclarans in the valley."

Karston's senses were reeling. Priest murder was a deadly sin among the men of the Rim worlds.

"When the war begins between the Rhad and Aurora, Karston," the general said quietly, "I shall intervene with an Imperial division. You know of the enclave the Navigators maintain on Aurora?"

Karston nodded dumbly.

"Do you know what they mine there?"

"Holy metals—"

"Holy metals indeed. Uranium. For nuclear bombs. Have you read your history? Do you know what brought the Dark Time?"

"Sin—"

"Fusion bombs. Open-ended nuclear weapons. Bombs that could smash whole continents. That is what the Navigators are doing on Aurora—mining the metals that will make those hell bombs possible again." The general's face was drawn, his voice savage.

Karston stared, not knowing what to say. The notion was almost impossible for him to grasp. For a hundred generations, men had gone in racial terror of the weapons that had destroyed the Golden Age.

"You will stop them, of course," he said in a shocked voice.

General Tran's eyes widened with surprise. "You are even

more provincial than I imagined, young Karston. *Stop* them? By the Star, of course not! I intend to have those weapons and the men who make them. When fate hands a man the power of a hundred suns, does he throw it away?" He began to laugh. The harsh sound grated on Karston's shattered nerves. "In recent times," Tran said, "the Empire has begun to be reinfected with an old, old virus. There's talk again about the rights of man, democracy, home rule for the provinces, the authority of the mob. All that has been tried too often and has failed too often. What's wanted is the rule of power, character, *order*. The Navigators aren't fit to dispose of the weapons of absolute mastery."

Karston stared hard at the Vegan. The sun was hot, but he felt the inward touch of an ancient, icy wind. "But you are," he said.

Tran drew a deep breath and looked out over the deceptive spring peace of the broad valley. His voice was harsh as the cutting edge of a sword as he asked, "Who else is there, Karston? When you see our great Galacton, you'll understand." Then he smiled swiftly and shook the younger man's shoulder with a surprisingly warm gesture. "Cheer up, young Karston. Who of the Gonlani-Rhad has ever been able to participate in the founding of a new age? Pray to your beatified Emeric to give you the strength to face greatness. With your help, I shall bring the Navigators down. You shall have your place in history."

His words filled Karston with dread.

Chapter Six

"If not in the holy dogma, nor yet in our command of the starships—then where, Grand Master, lies the strength of our Order?"
"In the searching minds and brave hearts of our young Navigators. Only there."
—Emeric of Rhada, Grand Master of Navigators,
The Dialogues, early Second Stellar Empire period

From out of the night of a million stars came our savage brother, man, and we found meaning. We also found death. So be it. This, too, will pass.
—Vulk lament, authorship unknown,
Interregnal period

Kynan awoke.

He had been dreaming that he had been in a battle on a rain-swept cliff far above the sea. In the dream he imagined he heard the death songs for Kreon, the star king; women's voices and the sound of muted battle horns. There had been some pain, too, but below the level of complete perception. Now he lay in a barely conscious peace, aware of the soothing comfort of a Vulk mind-touch.

He opened his eyes and saw the raftered ceiling of a familiar room. He was in his own chambers at Melissande. Firelight splashed the timbers and ancient stones. Through a partially open window, he could hear the sound of the Gonlan Sea.

He remembered. It had been no dream. Two priest-hating AbasNavs had tried to kill him on the track to Melissande.

"The war mare led us to you," a sibilant voice said.

Kynan turned his head to face the speaker. It was the Royal Vulk of Rhada—the mind-touch had told him as much—an ancient creature whose featureless skull shone pale in the firelight.

The young Navigator was fresh from Triad—that periodic mind-sharing between human Navigators and Vulks that was now an established part of the Order's ritual. The human-alien contact left the spirit refreshed and receptive and alert, needing little verbalization. Kynan's Triad had taken place on Omicron Lyri Nine with two young Vulks of the star king's court only a month ago. Consequently, thoughts flowed freely between himself and the alien mind.

"I am called Gret," the Vulk said.

"I know of you."

A warmth of feeling radiated from the creature. *And I of you, Kynan.*

Kynan's hand sought the place on his thigh where the priest-killer's lance had pierced him. The tissue was ridged; a fresh scar was forming. The Vulk had apparently healed him. He had heard that they had such powers, but he had been told that they could repair human tissue only in Triad. It was said that only when the minds of two Vulks and a human symbiote were in shared equilibrium could such "miracles" be wrought. Yet this single Vulk had closed his wound. He must be, Kynan thought wonderingly, incredibly old and wise.

Old enough, Navigator, the Vulk assured him. *Though I could do better with the help of my*—the concept was so alien that the human mind could only partially translate it into "mate"—*the Vulk Erit, she who shared herself with Ariane*—

Ariane! The young Navigator's romantic mind soared into realms of history and legend. This creature Gret bore the title of Royal Vulk in perpetuity, a gift from Kier, the second star king of Rhada, great-grandfather of the present old prince, Alberic. He had touched minds with Kier, and with his queen

Ariane, who had been a royal princess of the Empire, the daughter of Glamiss himself.

Through this creature's mind Kynan could, if the Vulk so desired it, return in spirit to the age of the great folk heroes of the Rhad. In spite of his present situation and because he was very young, Kynan felt sure that he would have been happier—possibly a folk hero himself—if he had lived in those great times—

He closed his eyes and began to slip into a dreaming sleep. But the Vulk said regretfully, "I would like to let you rest and dream, young Kynan. But it cannot be. Stay awake."

Kynan opened his eyes again. This time he regarded the Vulk more carefully. Though Vulks were so incredibly long-lived as to be virtually immortal on the human time scale, this one was actually beginning to show age. The slender body looked as though it consisted only of pale skin and corded muscle stretched over the delicate bone structure. The ridges of face and skull were clearly defined above the sensitive mouth, and the short kilt of metallic cloth hung loosely from the narrow, bladelike hips. The royal arms of the Rhadan Palatinate were embroidered on the creature's dark shirt, and he carried no weapons, only the customary Vulk lyre slung across his back.

The finely made lips formed a very human smile. *One day I will share Triad with you and Erit, and we will let you live those times we had with Kier the King and Ariane. Oh, they were thrilling days, young priest. I have lived so long among men that I know what pleasure it would give you to walk in the footsteps of my friend* (and here the human term was so enriched with love and devotion that Kynan almost felt the presence of the long-dead Kier, who was said to be the noblest of the Rhad).

The Vulk's thought continued to touch him, brushing like a wind across his mind. *But there is no time for that now.* A sadness, a gentle grief and compassion permeated the mind-touch. *Kreon, your bond-father, is dead.*

Tears sprang into Kynan's eyes. He was too late after all. The death song he had heard in his delirium had been real, too real.

With a delicacy typical of his kind, the Vulk withdrew his

mind from the grief in the young Navigator's, leaving only the gentle thought that family sorrow was a private thing. He said aloud, "I have the feeling that much died with Kreon—much that we should know. But it cannot be helped now. We must make the best of the situation as we find it."

Kynan felt a tremor of anger in his own breast. He might be an orphan by birth, unknown, of uncertain ancestry. But he was a man of Gonlan and a Rhad by adoption and conviction; bond-son to a Rhadan star king. He began to think of bloody revenge.

"*Was* it the Aurorans?" he asked.

The Vulk shrugged his narrow shoulders. "It happened on Aurora. That much is certain. That *only* is certain."

"And did they take my brother Karston?"

"Someone took your brother Karston," Gret said neutrally.

"What do Crespus and Baltus say?"

"What everyone says."

"And my father's minister? LaRoss?"

"All call for war."

For a moment Kynan felt a certain revulsion. The thought of war between dependencies of the Empire carried with it a taste of horror. One learned to respond that way if one followed the way of the Navigator. The Theocracy abhorred war between nations of men. It was the duty of all members of the Order to keep the peace of God, lest the Dark Time return again.

But Kynan was also a Rhad, and the men of the Rhadan worlds were warmen, fighters—perhaps the best fighters the Empire had. When provoked, they were terrible in battle. And even the Rhadan Navigators served their nation in times of battle.

The Vulk stood before the fire now, his lyre in his hand. Soft thrumming sounds came from the instrument. "I know what you feel, Kynan," he murmured. "Your love of family and Rhad honor are calling for blood. Yet you are a Navigator, and a Navigator lives to protect the way and the peace of God."

"We protect it with weapons when we must," Kynan said grimly.

"What do you know of history?" the Vulk asked.

"What all Navigators know," Kynan replied.

The Vulk strummed his lyre thoughtfully. "In the beginning —man's beginning, that is—there was the Dawn Age. This was before men left the Earth. There were endless wars in that time. Did you know that?"

"Little is known of that, Vulk. Our history begins with the First Empire."

"Far earlier than that, Kynan. There were four thousand Earth years to pass between the time men made their first flight to Earth's moon and their first journey to the nearest star. They not only had to learn to build starships—they had to learn to stop killing one another. That took much longer. The year one of the Galactic Era was the year 6,000 in the old calendar. So long it took for what we call the Golden Age to begin."

The Navigator sat on the edge of his pallet and studied the slender alien figure before the fire. "Even if all that is true—"

The Vulk struck a vibrant note. "Wait, let me go on. That Golden Age—the age of the First Stellar Empire—lasted for almost five thousand Earth years. And then the Empire fell, and the Dark Time began. No man knows how long the Interregnum lasted. The starships remained, as they may always remain, but men were savages. Only the Order kept the light of knowledge alive. *That* much history you know?"

"Of course."

"Then Glamiss left his home world of Vyka and began the reconquest. The time of hero-kings, Kynan, and great priests. These men were great because they had a vision far beyond their primitive learning. It is said in the Theocracy, is it not, that they saw the face of God?"

Kynan automatically make the sign of the Star. "We are so taught, Vulk."

"Glamiss Magnifico, and Kier, the Rebel of Rhada. Aaron, his father, and the beatified Emeric, Grand Master of the Order. These men built our Second Stellar Empire. Warmen of Gonlan, too, were at the last battle against the warlords. A second chance, Kynan. These men gave it to those who would come after." Gret turned his featureless face toward the young Navigator. "What was it they fought against? What was it that brought down the First Empire and began the Dark Time?"

Kynan replied from the dogma: "Sin. The forbidden weapons of science. The evil knowledge."

The Vulk shook his head. "A man would say so. But the Vulk know better, Kynan. Oh, how do the Vulk know!" The slender hands made nervous gestures on the lyre strings, and the air was filled with a grief-laden humming. "Since before the Dark Time, men have hunted and killed the Vulk, Kynan. Because we were *different*, because we shared the galaxy with man—only one small part of it in the beginning, to be sure, since we have never built machines—but even that brought the wrath of mankind down on us. You have studied the pogroms, you know how we were driven from place to place, death to death. And I tell you plainly, Kynan, it is this urge to kill and destroy—not the weapons he uses—that has haunted man since his beginnings. It was this that brought the Dark Time and every great evil."

"But men and Vulks have been—more than friends, *symbiotes* actually, for generations," protested the Navigator.

"Man hates what he loves and loves what he must kill. It is the nature of the creature," Gret said. "The most terrible predator ever spawned in the galaxy—that is man." The oddly articulated fingers drew a gentle melody from the lyre. "But magnificent, Kynan. *Magnificent,* truly. Man is everything the race of Vulks never became. That is why we return love for hatred, admiration for fear and contempt. There have always been men who understood this. This, and the nature of their own kind." The eyeless face glistened in the firelight. "At certain desperate times in man's history, such heroes must be found, or all that has been built in the last twelve thousand years will crumble away to final nothing." He moved closer to the young priest. "This is such a time, Kynan. And *you* must be such a man."

Kynan shook his head helplessly. "I am only a priest—a pilot of starships, Vulk. I don't understand you." The Navigator was filled with apprehension and self-doubt. Surely the ancient Vulk must understand that he was too young, too inexperienced, too *ignorant* to be involved in great events.

"Then listen. Open your mind to me. *Listen.*" The lyre gave forth strange quadratic sequences of humming sound that seemed to penetrate deep into the mind. Colored sounds, sounds with dimension and texture. Kynan resisted for a moment, overwhelmed by the power of the old Vulk's mental penetration. Jagged images appeared in his mind: Memories he *knew* were not his own; fragments of scenes he *knew* he could never have witnessed—

—the control room of a starship populated with five cowled figures that he somehow knew were princes of the Order. The chamber was familiar, for it was the bridge of an interstellar vessel. But the instruments were not the ancient consoles he understood. They were new and strange—

—the face of a man: cold-eyed and menacing with the assurance of the bigot, the fanatic. Imperial badges on his uniform. He stood in an audience chamber surrounded by ranks of warmen. AbasNavs. They raised their clenched fists and vowed to rid the Empire of priests. The man's name was Tran. He was the hero of Eridanus. He said, "I speak for the Galacton! The time of the Order is gone! The Navigators must be broken!" The gathered ranks roared. It was like the noise of beasts—

—a woman lay in childbirth in a tapestried, ornate room. The light of a single moon, cold and bright, shone through a mullioned window. A nurse held an infant, and a physician worked to bring forth a second child from the suffering woman. In the shadows, a cowled prince Navigator stood watching—

—a girl paced a narrow stone room. Janessa! She was much changed from the child who played at Star Field. She was desperate, weeping—and so beautiful. The legendary Ariane must have looked like that—!

There were other images, a tumbled profusion of them, spilling from the mind of the Vulk into Kynan's subconscious so rapidly that his forebrain could only note their strongest impressions: *A starfleet leaving Earth. The Navigator's enclave on Aurora. Armies debouching from the holy starships. His brother Karston's face, pale and irresolute. Escape—*

There was a wrenching sensation, a cry almost of mental pain. Kynan's eyes flew open, and he lay back against the wall, his head aching and throbbing.

The First Minister, LaRoss, was in the room. His face was dark as a thundercloud as he addressed the Royal Vulk. "What are you doing here, Master Gret? Kynan must rest. You know that."

The Vulk stood, head down, trembling with exhaustion. The translucent skin was livid with the terrible mental effort he had made.

LaRoss said sternly, "This is no time for Vulkish mysteries. The council will see you in the morning to assign you your command, Kynan. Gret—come with me."

Gret allowed himself to be led from the room, but as he reached the door, he turned and the thought exploded in Kynan's mind:

You know all you need to know. When the time comes, you will remember.

LaRoss's eyes narrowed, for he had caught the emotional content of the urgent command, though not its meaning.

"I would return now to Rhada," Gret said aloud, his voice thinned and weary. "I need to return."

Kynan heard LaRoss's reply, and it brought a chill into his blood. "I think for now you had better remain on Gonlan, Vulk."

He could hear no more, for the First Minister and the Vulk had moved down the passageway. But Gret's last thought, flung like a lance, struck him with a final urgency: *"Take the girl and go—NOW."*

Chapter Seven

The people cry, "Peace!" But there is no peace. The people cry, "Let us live!" But they die. The princes are wolves and the Empire dies and the wars devour us! This is the Dark Time. Spirits of darkness, have mercy on our souls!

—Chant from *The Book of Warls*,
Interregnal period

One more such victory and we are undone.
—Attributed to Glamiss of Vyka,
founder of the Second Stellar Empire,
after the Battle of Karma

Janessa, heiress of Aurora, studied the phosphorescent waves of the Gonlan Sea crashing on the rocks far below. In the moonless dark, the wind-created swells, with a thousand empty miles behind them, shattered into glowing spindrift against the coast of the Stoneland Peninsula. Soaring night birds, unseen in the stormy sky, gave mournful cries. Their voices made the girl's flesh prickle. It was like listening to the dead voices of cybs and demons.

Sighing, she closed the window, and for a moment her own

reflection looked back at her, limned against the ocean darkness. She was a slender girl, tall for her age, which was eighteen Standard Years (twelve of her home planet's long seasons). Her hair was straight and silvery blond, held with a tiara of green stones, the deep royal color of Aurora.

Ever since childhood she had dreamed of visiting Gonlan and the Palatinate; even the capital world of Rhada. But she had never, in her deepest nightmares, imagined that she would come to this wild and primitive planet as a prisoner. She was the daughter of the Elector of Aurora, a noblewoman of the Empire. And yet, here she was, mewed up in a stone tower like a storybook princess, but without the storybook princess's hope of rescue. She bit her lips and refused to cry, but it was not easy.

As in a dream, she remembered the sudden, savage violence that had shattered the decorum of her betrothal ceremonies. The well-drilled companies of warmen invading Star Field, moving swiftly and mercilessly among the guests with sword and flail.

She wondered if her father, the Elector, was still alive. Had he managed to rally his surprised troops and drive the invaders away? And Karston—what had happened to her handsome promised husband? Something dreadful, surely, else the men of Gonlan would not have taken her hostage— She frowned and shivered with outraged dignity. *Hostage.* An Auroran hostage on Gonlan! It seemed almost beyond belief. Yet here she was, with armed warmen at her door. She swept the water jug from the serving table in a sudden fury. *The warmen of Aurora will come and take this Melissande apart stone by stone,* she thought, raging.

She sat suddenly on the narrow bed and rubbed her naked arms. It seemed to have grown very cold. She thought about her actual situation, and a heaviness grew in her breast. The warmen of Aurora might come. Then again, they might not. The Aurorans were the least warlike of the Rim dwellers. Good people, too. They would only be confused and discomfited by this sudden stroke of disaster. She could make no sense of it herself. To attack a betrothal ceremony was insane, meaningless.

And now, she had heard the death songs for a star king. Did that mean that Kreon was dead? Kreon, the marvelous old warrior who called her his daughter and spoke of the time to come when she would give him grandchildren, kings to rule in Gonlan some day?

No one had come to her to tell her the meaning of the death songs. Only Baltus, the warlock, had come to question her and see to her comfort. But he had been closemouthed, refusing to comment on her demand to be heard by Kreon, refusing even to carry her message to Alberic of Rhada, Gonlan's overlord.

She was a prisoner, cut off from the world outside. Why, the Empire could fall and she wouldn't even know of it!

"I'll have their heads on a pike for this," she told herself, holding back the tears angrily. "And their guts for garters." That was an expression her father always used when he was angry. She thought about him, surrounded by young warmen, stripped of his power. In her imagination she saw Star Field burning, handsome Karston lying dead, herself orphaned and widowed even before marriage—

It was too much. Janessa of Aurora threw herself on the spartan bed and wept.

She had very nearly wept herself into exhaustion when the locks on her door rattled. She had barely time to stand defiantly before a young man in black clericals appeared.

Kynan. It was years since she had seen the star king's bondson. She remembered him as a thin, rather intense young boy who talked only of commanding starships and other religious matters. Now suddenly the boy stood before her, grown into a well-favored warman, in the black of the Order of Navigators.

She had seen no friendly face since being locked up here in this place; save only for the warlock, she had seen no one at all but her guards. Her grief and anger left her, and she allowed herself a moment of hope. Kynan, a holy Navigator and bond-kin to the star king, would surely set things right now.

Kynan, for his part, was suddenly stricken mute by the blond beauty of his brother's almost-betrothed. He remembered her only as an adolescent girl playing in the gardens at Star Field.

They both spoke at once. Then the girl, better trained in the amenities, inclined her head for a formal blessing and made the sign of the Star.

"Janessa," Kynan said. "I'm sorry to find you here."

The girl's eyes flashed with sudden anger. "No sorrier than I to be here, Nav Kynan."

Kynan frowned. He had come to her quickly, driven by powers he did not fully understand, yet powers that he trusted completely. The Royal Vulk's instructions had been direct and compelling. He knew enough about the Vulk mind-touch to understand that the reasons implanted in his subconscious by Gret would surface with time to rest and consider. He also knew that he would not act, even on the urgings of the Vulk of Rhada, if the reasons imbedded in his personality by the alien were improper or repugnant to his spirit and personality. He felt no such reservations, only a deep and anxious urgency.

"I must take you out of here, Janessa. To do it, I need your absolute obedience and cooperation."

"Out?" Janessa suppressed the hope that rose in her with skepticism. "Out past five hundred warmen—all, apparently, now my enemies?"

"We can manage it, with luck. I am a Navigator and the king's bond-son," Kynan said, with a touch of youthful bravado.

"Take me only as far as Kreon, Kynan," Janessa pleaded. "I haven't been allowed even to see the star king."

The Navigator's face sobered beneath the dark round thatch of his hair. "Didn't you hear the death songs and the war horns?"

Janessa's heart felt cold. "He's dead? The old king is really dead?"

"Murdered," Kynan said.

"No Auroran killed him!" the girl said with spirit.

"I believe that. The Rhad Vulk believes it, too. But we are the only ones who do. LaRoss and Tirzah have ordered General Crespus to prepare a strike force against Aurora."

The girl stepped closer to the Navigator and protested. "Kynan, you must not let them do it'!"

"I am not certain I can prevent it, Janessa. I am a bond-son, not the true heir to Gonlan. That's why we must leave here."

"And go where?"

"With luck, to the Order's enclave on Aurora. I have no authority to go there, but neither I nor Gret see any alternative. Somehow, the priest-killers are behind all this. We feel it."

Janessa walked to the window and stood for a moment regarding the Navigator. This talk of "we" meant that he was fresh from—if not full Triad—at least mind-touch with the Royal Vulk. Janessa, like many of the inhabitants of the Empire, still feared the strange Vulks. She knew that Navigators went regularly into Triad with them, and Rhadans generally did the same, though not so often. It was, in fact, this policy of Rhad-Vulk integration that had prevented Aurora, in Kier the Rebel's time, from becoming a part of the Rhadan Palatinate. Yet, she thought, to her certain knowledge, no harm had ever come to a human from a Vulk. She must not permit her inbred Auroran prejudice to impair her trust in Kynan, who was a priest of the Order—and, incidentally, a very handsome young man. That thought brought a touch of color to her cheeks, and she tossed her head so that the long straight fall of her hair shimmered in the torchlight.

Kynan, for his part, had been studying the girl. She looked steady enough; strong enough, too, for what could only be a hellishly difficult journey to the spaceport. She had been wearing court dress when she was abducted from Star Field. But someone, perhaps the Navigator commanding the Rhad starship that brought her to Gonlan, had seen to it that she received more serviceable clothing, for the climate of the Gonlan coast was severe. Now Janessa's slender figure was encased in the tights, leotard, and kilt of a Rhadan cadet. Except for her hair, one might almost take her for a page or an ensign of the castle garrison. Almost—not entirely. Janessa, for all her athletic slenderness, was unmistakably female. And Navigators were *not* celibates.

As if to chastise himself for his thoughts, Kynan said, "If you'll cooperate with me, we'll try to stop this insanity before it's started—and bring you safely to my brother." Whose wife she was destined to be by agreement, custom, and tradition, Kynan thought. Remember *that*.

"I will obey you, of course, Nav Kynan," she said formally, the color still in her cheeks. There was a strange rapport between them that she sensed now, very strongly. She knew with great certainty that he had been admiring her, and it both disturbed and excited her.

"The Lyri starship that brought me to Gonlan should still be in Gonlanburg. It wasn't to leave until tomorrow morning. I'll go now and raid the stable for horses. If we can get away from Melissande within the hour, there should be time."

And then, because he suddenly realized that he had been giving orders to a noblewoman of the Empire, who was also a very attractive girl, he paused in some confusion.

"It is for the best, Lady Janessa. You mustn't stay here," he said. "Will you make ready?"

"I will do anything you say, Nav Kynan," Janessa replied with unaccustomed humility."

Kynan bowed and withdrew, wondering why it was that, in spite of the perilousness of the situation, he felt light-hearted.

But once in the lower levels of Melissande, Kynan's Janessa-induced euphoria began to fade. The guardrooms and barracks were filling with warmen—the individual soldiers gathering their kits for a protracted off-world campaign. Those who recognized him as the returned bond-son of the warleader paused in their activities to salute him, and here and there he would encounter one more religious than the rest who would make the sign of the Star in request of a benediction before battle.

Kynan tried to estimate how long it would be before General Crespus would be able to assemble a complete strike force for an attack on Aurora. The Rhad were warlike and organized for battle, but all the Rhadan worlds were more or less primitive when compared to the Inner Planets, where Kynan had recently been serving. It would take more time to assemble an expedition here than, say, in the Lyra province, where communications were swifter.

Thirty-six hours would be a reasonable guess, he thought. A

day and a half to assemble the first elements of a strike. The bulk of the Gonlani star fleet would be off-world at this moment, but he had no doubt that the starships within the Rhadan volume of space would already have been recalled to the home planet for troop-carrier duty with the levies. The first of them would be arriving within hours. The Lyri starship that had been his, and that had brought him home, might already have been requested to clear the port of Gonlanburg to make room for the homecoming vessels. Kynan prayed that Brother Evart, to whom he had turned over command, would be as deliberate in making his plans for departure as he was in performing his other holy offices.

As the young Navigator made his way deeper into the bowels of the sprawling castle-hunting lodge toward the stables, the images planted in his mind by the Rhadan Vulk began to surface. The facts, if facts they were, surprised him; their intellectual and emotional inferences, however, did not. Many times, after undergoing Triad both in the Theocracy and later in Lyra, Kynan had attempted to rationalize the peculiar effect of the experience.

For several generations now, humans had been undergoing the symbiotic experience of Triad with the ancient Vulks. Much of what men knew of their own history was learned in this way, for Vulks lived extraordinarily long lives. But far more significant than the simple interflow of information among Vulk and human minds during the experience was the emotional rapport established. In the Dark Time—and even before, during the Golden Age of the First Empire—men had feared and hated the Vulk simply for being *different*. But with the growth of the Triad experience, sanctioned by the Order of Navigators only in the last century, a new depth and dimension had been added to human domination of the old worlds of the Empire.

It was, for example, only since Triadism that men had begun to understand that the Empires, First *and* Second, were stellar rather than truly galactic—that is, that the outposts of human power were scattered throughout the known galaxy, but that they in no way dominated the immense star-cloud known as the Milky Way. The Vulk were the only intelligent life-form men had ever discovered in the galaxy. But the actual number of habitable worlds visited by either Stellar Empire was minute compared to the number existing. This concept alone was both sobering and instructive to men.

But the important consideration was that a man who had undergone the experience of Triad could *accept* such a diminishing fact *emotionally* because the Vulk, a far calmer people than humanity, accepted it with grace and thoughtful caution rather than with alarm.

Thus it was that Gret could charge Kynan's subconscious with a set of the most disturbing facts, secure in the knowledge that he would respond to each emerging bit of information calmly and without shock

Item. *The AbasNavs who attempted to kill him on the sea cliffs had been employed by someone within the household of Melissande.* Somehow, Gret *knew* this. And Kynan knew it now. Had he learned it from any source other than the Vulk's mind-touch, he would have been infuriated and alarmed. He was not. It was simply a fact—to be evaluated and put into perspective among other facts, after which a course of action must be devised.

Item. *Kynan was under periodic scrutiny—by what means he did not know—of powerful members of the Order.* This would probably not have surprised or alarmed Kynan in any case. As a junior priest of a great Order, he expected ghostly supervision by his superiors. What *was* remarkable was that Gret knew (and so, therefore, did Kynan now) that he, Kynan, was considered important to the watchers.

Item. *The Vulk, grown old in the practice of statecraft, believed that the war between Aurora and Gonlan was being fomented to excuse Imperial intervention. If Rhada supported her vassal state Gonlan, the war would engulf the entire Rim. The Order's enclave on Aurora was the key.*

Kynan frowned. His head ached with unaccustomed thought. He was after all, he told himself, only a small priest of the Order of Navigators. His business was the piloting of holy vessels, not interstellar intrigue and politics.

But he was a Rhad by adoption, a member of the royal house of Gonlan by bond and affection and now protector (self-appointed) of the princess and heiress of Aurora. If great affairs pivoted on him in ways he did not understand, let them. He would do his duty as a priest, as a man, and as a citizen of the Empire.

The high-flown phrases sounded a bit absurd to him as he made his way into the stable court. What he was actually planning at the moment was horse-stealing and illegal flight with a prisoner of the government of Gonlan—which could earn him the rank of traitor in addition to all the rest.

It had been so long since he had been home that none of the war mares in the court recognized him—none but the old beast who had carried him from Gonlanburg. He called her in the darkness.

"Ky-nan." Tigerish teeth, once needle-sharp but worn down with age, nipped at his shoulder in greeting.

Fresh from his mind-contact with Gret, Kynan could feel clearly the savage affection emanating from the animal. He was the one familiar inhabitant of the castle, and the old mare, bedded down with the younger mounts of the warmen of Melissande, had been lonely.

He touched her gray muzzle gently, breathing in the rank smell of the stable and the tang of fresh blood. The animals had only just been given their daily meal of newly slaughtered game.

The other war horses, mostly mares because the stallions were well-nigh unmanageable, began to mill about restlessly. They recognized him as a Rhadan and one who belonged at Melissande, but he was unfamiliar to them, and this made them restless.

"We go?" the old mare asked, tossing her head. "We go fight now?"

Kynan had planned to steal other horses. Younger and stronger animals might very well be needed for the flight across the desolate Stoneland Peninsula to Gonlanburg. But the mare's entreaty touched him. She had seen better days, and he knew that some warman, perhaps needing a stronger mount and lacking the money to buy her a hunt-pasture, had had to sell her to the hack renter at the spaceport. Now her adventure on the cliffs was fresh in her mind, and she imagined she was once again a warman's charger.

"Skua—will—fight," she breathed restlessly.

"Skua. Is that your name?"

"Yes, yes." She stamped impatiently, remembering old battles.

Kynan made a decision. It was probably unwise, but, he reflected, many an austere superior had remarked on his impulsiveness, and he was still alive, still functioning as a priest-Navigator. One must allow instinct free rein sometimes, he reminded himself. Skua would do as a mount for Janessa. "Yes," he told the mare. "Soon we go." He searched the milling horse herd for another mount and found one, a tall and silvery mare rolling her eyes nervously at him.

He caught her attention and commanded her to come to him. Skua made jealous noises, and he quieted her with a touch. The silver mare stood dancing before him. "Not—my —master," she muttered, backing.

She was difficult to dominate, but he held an image in his mind: a stretch of beach below the seawall. He gave both animals the strongest commands he could manage, picturing in detail the causeway across the defensive ditches, the low wall of the horse paddock, the winding path to the sea.

While he did this, he busied himself with light saddles taken from the saddletrees lining the walls. He was able to equip Skua without trouble, but the silver mare still resisted him, her mind a confusion of baffled loyalty and his explicit commands.

"You will go there," he said to the young mare.

She shook her head and half reared, setting the stirrups to swinging against her sweating flanks. For a moment Kynan despaired of being able to control her sufficiently to make her comply with his orders. But old Skua, her patience at an end and her jealousy aroused, slashed angrily at the young mare with a clawed forefoot. For a moment the two animals glared furiously at one another, and Kynan thought that a battle must surely begin between them. Then Skua's age and experience overbore the young beast's energetic anxiety, and the silvery head lowered and bobbed in submission.

Kynan breathed a deep sigh of relief and slapped at Skua's flank. "You go now. To the sea. Wait for me."

Skua butted the silver mare into action, herding her toward the opening of the paddock. Kynan watched as they vanished into the night. A movement near the staircase descending from the upper levels made him turn, reaching for his pistol. But there was nothing visible. His heart raced, and he heard the watch calling the half hour before midnight. He shoved his way through the restless horse herd toward the stairs. He must free Janessa now and reach Gonlanburg before first light.

Chapter Eight

I concluded that our holy Order had the responsibility to return to the people of the worlds a voice in their own destiny. I preached that the power of the star kings was not absolute and that the rights of the Galacton were his only so long as the people desired his rule. To this end I sought to unlock the ancient mysteries. This, too, I recant. Democracy lies far in the future.
—Navigator Anselm Styr's confession on the scaffold at Biblios Brittanis, Mars, early Second Stellar Empire period

I am the law. You are only the Galacton.
—Attributed to General Alain Veg Tran (to Torquas the Poet), middle Second Stellar Empire period

The great starship lay in the umbra of Gonlan, an immense dark shape against the sparse starfields of the galactic Rim. In the control room, the Five still watched their instruments.

"He did not reach Kreon. The plan is breaking down," the Tactician said.

The Preacher, sensing an opening for theology among these worldly princes of the Order, said heavily, "No plan can operate exactly as men devise it, brothers. The hand of God works in mysterious ways."

The Psychologist sighed. "No plan has ever worked without a bit of help. We will simply have to take the longer way. If he had reached Kreon in time, it would have been easier to resolve. The Vulk very nearly did our work for us."

The Logician studied the symbols that had replaced the holographic figures on his console screen. "We must not rely too heavily on the Vulk. Remember they have a strangely tolerant attitude, and they rely too heavily on the nature of men. Gret has always been a libertarian at heart. All Vulks are."

"It is not my field," the Technician remarked, "but I have always understood that the plan envisioned a democratic endpoint."

"Too much too soon is worse than nothing at all," the Tactician said brusquely. "This stage is simply meant to protect the Order, not to give a franchise to every peasant on every backwater world."

The Logician gave a short, unpleasant laugh. "Let us at least be honest with one another. This stage of the plan is intended to make the Order and the Imperial power one. No more than that, and certainly no less."

The Tactician responded sharply, with military intolerance. "Are you suggesting at this point that the plan is wrong?"

The Psychologist intervened swiftly. "Enough, now. No one questions the value of the plan. But the boy didn't reach Kreon in time, and the Vulk has mind-touched him. Variables are being introduced more quickly than we can cope with them. The important thing is to get him to Nyor at once. Can you guide him, Technician?"

The Technician shook his head. "The Vulk has interfered with his conditioning. I can't break through the mind-touch."

"What of the girl?"

"She was implanted with a locator, nothing more."

"Thank the Star for that, at any rate," the Logician said. "At least we can follow them."

"Quite helplessly, I'm afraid," the Technician said. "My

contact with him has been distorted badly ever since the Vulk touched him. Now there is no way of interfering."

The Logician said impatiently, "To make the plan function, we must have a confrontation. It is imperative."

"Don't despair of the plan. Torquas will surely be with Tran when the good General plunges into the situation on Aurora."

"Don't be too sure of that," the Logician said. "Torquas prefers poems to battles. Tran will probably handle Aurora alone."

The Psychologist said, "An agent in Saclara says our contact has been murdered by Tran's AbasNav Vegans."

The Preacher nodded as though expecting this information. "He was piloting a holy vessel. Whatever he learned was under the seal of service. He was going to report it to us, and the hand of God has struck him down."

"Nonsense," the Tactician snapped testily. "The hand of *Tran* struck him down because he suspected where a priest's higher duty lies. *With the Order.*"

"Nevertheless," the Psychologist said, "his information failed to reach us. Logician—can you make an educated guess what it might have been?"

"Partially, only that."

"Well, then?"

"That Karston is on Earth—very probably at Saclara."

"A sorry awakening for him," the Preacher said sadly. "To have bought disaster at the price of one's own father."

"These Rim princes are a grasping lot," the Tactician said. "No price is too great for them to pay for a little power."

The Psychologist smiled mirthlessly. "And are we so different, brother?"

The Tactician retorted smartly, "We fight for the Order."

"Yes, well at the moment we don't fight at all," the Psychologist murmured. "Everything rides with a twenty-year-old boy. And we can only watch."

"I have them again," the Technician said, working on his instruments.

The Five gave their attention to the display consoles. The images were dark and indistinct, doll figures moving through a microcosmic storm of wind and rain.

"By the Star!" the Technician breathed. "There is someone waiting for them on the beach."

"The Vulk?" demanded the Tactician.

The Technician shook his cowled head. "No. It is Baltus, the star king's warlock."

The Five bent to the consoles, watching and waiting.

With the towering, dark bulk of Melissande behind them, Kynan and Janessa made their way down the twisting path to the sea. They had managed to move through the back passageways and corridors of the ancient stone keep without arousing pursuit—for Kynan remembered Melissande well. But there had been no possibility of taking Janessa from her tower apartments out of sight of the young warman put by her door to guard her; this man Kynan had simply overborne with both his priesthood and his position as a member of the royal house of Gonlan. But it was inevitable that the soldier would check with his captain when Janessa was not promptly returned, and when this happened, the troops would be turned out to search for her.

The wind, racing aross a thousand kilometers of open ocean from the ice barrier far to the north, was frigid with polar rain. The path, steeply descending the rock cliffs, was dangerously slippery. Once Janessa stumbled, and he had to turn and hold her until she regained her balance. The warmth of her against him set his heart to racing. He could scarcely see her face in the stormy night, but he felt her wet hair blowing against his cheek. "All right?" he said.

"Yes," she breathed, "but hurry. They'll be after us soon."

He turned and continued down the path. He could hear the sound of the surf now, very clearly. He hoped desperately that the mare Skua had found her way to this place. Without horses they would be hopelessly trapped against the sea. And what he could say by way of explanation to Crespus and LaRoss would save neither Janessa nor himself. With Kreon dead, his position among the nobility of Gonlan was anomalous. Only those who chose to honor the old star king's bond-relatives need do so; no longer were free men bound to be guided by the hand of a dead king.

The path began to level now, and Kynan could feel the gritty depth of sand beneath his feet. But the wind was turbulent here, billowing against the base of the sheer cliffs, and it was necessary to shield one's face against the stinging lash of the driven spray.

Kynan heard, over the roar of the wind and sea, the cry of the mare Skua, and soon her slender bulk stood between him and the slashing spray. Janessa pressed close behind, and Kynan said in her ear, "I didn't think the storm would be this bad. It may drive the sea against the cliffs."

Gonlan's seas were without tides, for the planet had no satellites. But the howling equinoctal storms often piled the waters against the sheer cliffs of the Stoneland Peninsula, covering the narrow strands of beach at the base of the palisades.

"We might be trapped here?" Janessa asked.

It could be far worse than that, Kynan knew. Rhadan mares were strong swimmers; even they could brave the fury of this storm for only short distances. But he said with a confidence he did not feel, "We'll stay on the beach only a short time. I know these cliffs. There's a trail we can use to get to the plateau about two kilometers from here."

The mare tossed her head and said warningly, "Ky-nan. Go. Go now."

Kynan rubbed the soft, storm-wet muzzle and said, "Yes, now." He turned to help Janessa mount and saw the other shapes in the darkness. The silver mare was moving toward him across the strand, but behind her came still another animal, this one carrying a man whose cape, wind-driven, stood out like a black banner. Kynan drew his pistol, aimed, and fired.

The flint spark sputtered across the priming pan and died. The pistol was useless in this drenching rain. Kynan dropped it and drew his sword from the scabbard across his back.

The mounted man pulled up short and raised his open hands. He said, "Kynan."

The Navigator knew that voice: his bond-father's warlock, Baltus.

"Get down," Kynan shouted, his words whipped away into the night by the storm.

The warlock slipped from his charger and came near. Kynan kept the point of his sword against the old man's chest. "I heard you instruct the mare in the stable court," the warlock said.

"You can't stop us, Baltus," Kynan said. "Why did you come here?"

The warlock inclined his head toward Janessa: a touch of courtliness that seemed to Kynan wildly out of place on this rain-lashed, dark stretch of ocean beach.

"He is unarmed, Kynan," Janessa said.

"Why have you come here?" Kynan demanded again. "Are you alone?"

"Yes, Nav Kynan. But we had better leave this place quickly."

Kynan frowned in a fury of indecision. But the warlock was right. Even as they spoke, he could feel the force of the wind increasing. Soon they could be overwhelmed by the piling of the sea against the cliffs. Kynan made his choice. He had known from the moment the pistol misfired that he could not kill his bond-father's warlock in cold blood.

"All right," he said tightly. "Mount up. But you'll explain, Baltus. And keep your hands where I can see them."

"I will explain willingly, Nav Kynan," the warlock said, "when we've put Melissande well behind us."

Kynan called the silver mare and mounted. The warlock swung onto his animal. Kynan looked back along the steep path to the place where the massive bulk of Melissande lay hidden in the wild darkness. There were no signs of pursuit yet.

He reversed his sword and handed it to Janessa. "Ride behind him," he said. "If he tries to leave us, use this."

The girls fingers closed over the hilt, but Kynan could not see the expression on her face. He felt harried and not in control of the situation. He knew that the girl would be no more willing to strike down the old warlock than he was. Yet there was nothing else he could do but chance the dangers of the developing situation. The silver mare danced under him and rolled her eyes at the encroaching sea.

"Follow me now," Kynan shouted, and guided the procession along the narrowing strand of beach at a gallop. The waves were crashing against the scattered boulders at the cliff base, and he hoped desperately that he had not waited too long.

Chapter Nine

Though I wear a crown of stars and comets and my word is law on worlds I have never seen; and though I command great fleets and armies and men fear me and obey—yet my truest pleasure is to know that men everywhere sing my songs. What greater legacy could I leave to my people? Art is love, and love is all.
—Torquas the Poet, *The Eroticon*,
middle Second Stellar Empire

By the middle years of the Torquan Dynasty, the Empire had broken the absolute power of the feudal star kings. Throughout the Imperium, the forces of home rule and popular democracy were stirring. But the power wrested from the provincial kings was not yet free to be delivered into the hands of the citizens of the Empire. It lay now in the mailed fist of the Empire and the only slightly gentler hand of the Order. This was the situation extant as the forces of Gonlan and Aurora mobilized to fight the first civil war in a century.
—Nav (Bishop) Julianus Mullerium,
Anticlericalism in the Age of the Star Kings,
middle Second Stellar Empire period

* * *

The city of Nyor at evening time was one of the magnificent sights of the known galaxy. Time out of mind the capital of the Empire had stood on the island between the two rivers; as the tides of history swept over it again and again, it had expanded and contracted like a living organism. In the Dark Time it had been a keep and a few blocks of hovels atop its ancient tel—a massive mound of earth enriched with uncounted layers of archeological debris; the heritage of aeons of human occupation. But now, in the reign of the last of the Torquans, the city stood sheathed in colored marble and exotic building stones brought from worlds across the galaxy. White colonnades and crystal towers caught the fading light of the sun. Warmen from the farthest provinces of the Empire patrolled the walls and terraces of the citadel, the streets and gardens of the city proper.

The Nyori, for uncounted centuries the most cynical and suspicious townsmen in the Empire, were in this twilight of the great star kings' age, enjoying an unparalleled prosperity and peace. Two thousand planets were now subject to the House of Vyka, and their wealth poured into this greatest of the Empire's cities.

In the reign of Torquas IX, who had died in a starship accident at the age of six, and in the reign of Torquas X, whom men referred to as the Heretic, the Empire Tower had been incorporated into the grounds of the citadel. This incredibly old structure was said to be a part of the original city of Nyor, and it now descended a full kilometer into the rubbled mound of the tel on which the modern city stood. The detritus of millennia and fully a thousand sackings had built the tel into a series of quite respectable hills, so that the capital of the Second Stellar Empire stood in many places high above the placid waters of the two rivers.

The upper levels of the Tower had been extended into stepped terraces supported by graceful flying buttresses and tapering columns; in this time the building resembled a golden honeycomb atop a massive base. The Tower's lower levels were still used as a prison, as the entire structure had been in the time of Glamiss Magnifico and his son Torquas I. But the highest stories now served as the favorite residence for the present Galacton and his court.

It was here that General Veg Tran found his ruler and sovereign, Torquas, thirteenth of that name, Galacton, King of the Universe, Protector of the Faith, Defender of the Inner and Outer Marches, Commander of the Starfleets, Beloved of the Star, Lord of Nyor and Hereditary Warleader of Vyka—whom some men called the Poet, and others the Fool.

On that spring evening, the court was enjoying a show of changing patterns of light. Even as he strode across the polished marble of the fiftieth level of the Tower, Alain Veg Tran could hear the shouts of laughter, the drugged giggles, the steely music and shrill singing that accompanied the Galacton's pleasures.

The light shows were usually given in the Galacton's private chambers, where, at considerable expense, the Royal Chamberlain had constructed an immense uterine cave devoid of windows and muffled with a strident mélange of changeable colored draperies. The light projectors were electric, products of the royal warlocks' workshops, and it was claimed for them that they could project a different series of light patterns each half hour for the next three hundred years without repeating themselves.

Whether or not they did repeat themselves was, however, of very little moment to Torquas and his giggling companions, for light shows were enjoyed (by specific order of the Galacton) only when the audience was completely drugged with hemp. "It heightens the perceptions," Torquas declared, "allowing closer communion with the oversoul." If the King of the Universe saw it this way, there could be no argument in Nyor. Light shows and hallucinogens were *de rigueur* in the city now. Cheap versions of the Galacton's pleasures were for sale in every tavern and public house along the Great Street.

General the Honorable Alain Veg Tran, attended by a resplendently uniformed officer of the Vegan Imperials, paused for a moment in the anteroom, listening to the sounds of revelry from the Galacton's theater chamber.

"How long has this one lasted, Captain?" he asked the Vegan warman.

The soldier's dark eyes were amused under the feathered circlet of his dress helmet. "Only two days, Leader."

"Has he seen anyone from the Rim?"

"He's done nothing but listen to that electric squealing and smoke hemp for the last forty-eight hours." The praetorian's lip curled slightly. "The Auroran Commissioner has been cooling his heels for a week."

Veg Tran listened for a moment to the amplified dissonances echoing from the Galacton's chambers. The Imperial Commissioner for Aurora was a well-intentioned but ineffectual bureaucrat. News of the attack on Aurora would reach the Galacton only through channels approved by Veg Tran—which, with a fool for a sovereign, was the only proper way.

"I'll see him now," Tran said.

"It's a howling madhouse in there, Leader. You'll need earplugs," the soldier said.

"Inform all members of the General Staff that there is to be a meeting in my town house at the twentieth hour. No excuses will be acceptable. I want them there."

"Sir." The Vegan saluted and withdrew. Veg Tran walked slowly toward the sounds of nightmare revelry.

At the door, two Lyri guardsmen clashed their weapons in salute and opened the violently decorated portals.

Veg Tran stepped into a maelstrom of colored light, movement, smoke, and noise. The occupants of the vast room were all young, in their teens and twenties: the Galacton's playmates, the general thought sardonically. It was impossible to be certain in the confusion of shifting colors and shadows, but there were certainly more than a hundred young people in the room. Some lay on the pillowed floor in drugged stupor. Others recited poems or sang songs unlistened to. Still others danced, their eyes half hooded in a euphoric daze. Every sort of costume imaginable was displayed: feathers, metallic cloths, native costumes from the far worlds, mad variations of uniforms and current styles. Many of the young people had discarded all clothing and danced or writhed in time to the dissonances as the fragments of colored light painted their skins with swiftly changing patterns.

Veg Tran picked his way through the crowd, ignoring the

advances of dazed celebrants. In the center of the room, sprawled on a stepped dais, lay the Galacton. He was playing a stringed instrument, and it was his music that was being amplified to earsplitting howls and twangs by the machines built for him by the warlocks in the workshop.

All around Torquas his friends and sycophants sat, squatted, or reclined. Some, perhaps sincerely affected by the music, waved their hands and arms in flying motions. Others merely sat, mouths agape in the attitude of mindless appreciation Torquas had let be known had his approval.

The Galacton himself was dressed in a silver cape and bronze codpiece. His hair and beard were long and dressed carefully into an artificial *déshabillé*. Tiny platinum bells had been woven into his locks and whiskers, and their penetrating sound could be heard punctuating each undisciplined strophe of the music he was playing.

He regarded Veg Tran for some time before recognition came into his hemp-fogged eyes. Tran suppressed a scowl of disgust and merely stood, waiting. Instead of a Vyk warrior of twenty, which was what Torquas was—he looked like some strangely desexed girl. The bells pinged and tinkled as the Galacton turned his head and raised his arms for silence. The gathered celebrants subsided into a murmuring confusion.

"General," the Galacton said, with a white smile. "General —how good of you to join us in the worship of the galactic spirit."

A few of the more nearly coherent young nobles muttered, "Amen," and made the currently popular variation on the sign of the Star. It was a gesture no Navigator would have recognized, Veg Tran thought wryly. But then the Galacton's playmates plunged into a new religion—or *religious experience* as they liked to say—each week.

"An occasion," the Galacton said with a shrill laugh. "I shall compose a poem in the general's honor."

The celebrants shouted approval. The current vogue was for what Torquas called *spontaneous vapidity*. This consisted mainly of art springing unconfined from souls freed of convention by various drugs. "The art of the void," Torquas called it. "Art created to be forgotten."

Now he struck a painfully dissonant "accidental" chord from his electric strings and began to create.

> "Warlike man lies fallow in the night of space between
> The stars,
> Yet love speaks to us all and we listen
> To its sensual voice
> After all.
> Iron man with an iron heart and a head of iron
> Too,
> Why have you come into the womb of night to
> Disturb us?"

He struck another chord to indicate that the poem was ended. An empty-faced child lying at his feet writhed and began to weep. "Oh, Leader—oh, Torquas, how beautifully you speak our thoughts!" The others took up the cry, laughing or weeping or applauding as the mood struck them. Or, thought Tran contemptuously, as they thought the mood struck Torquas.

When the clamor had died slightly, the Galacton shouted to Tran, "That was for you, General. In your honor."

Tran inclined his head slightly and said, "I am touched, Torquas."

"I am glad you are, General. It isn't often a *military* man can school himself to appreciate art," the Galacton said. "Have you come to join us then?"

Tran stepped to the dais and seated himself beside the Galacton. Torquas's platinum bells pinged delicately as he moved to make room. Tran said, "Not this time, King."

Torquas's face collapsed into a pouting frown. "There's trouble somewhere. You only come here when there's some sort of unpleasantness. What is it now?"

"I am taking my own division and some Vyks to the Rim, King," the Vegan said. "There *is* some trouble, I'm afraid."

"I knew it," the Galacton said, shoving the electric lyre from him so that it hummed and twanged on the lightswirling floor. He raised his voice angrily. "All of you. Get out. Get out now."

The celebrants began to withdraw, those able to walk

assisting those too far gone in hemp to move.

Torquas said in a complaining voice, "How can one be *free* when there is always some trouble somewhere? How can *love* prevail? Answer me that, General. Answer me that, please." Then before Veg Tran could speak, he raised his voice to shout at the unseen light-projector operators. "Stop the lights! Stop them, I say! I don't want the lights any more!"

The dazzling movement of colors slowed and finally halted. Torquas, his face limned in red, green, and purple, stared at Veg Tran with glistening, tear-filled eyes. Hemp made the Galacton weep easily.

"It isn't as bad as that, Torquas," Veg Tran murmured. "A squabble on the Rim. There is no need for you to concern yourself."

"But you'll be *fighting*."

This, Tran thought, *is a direct descendant of Glamiss, who conquered Vyka and then the known galaxy.*

"Who is it?" the Galacton demanded. "Who is it *this* time?"

"Gonlan and Aurora."

"Gonlan is part of Rhada, isn't it?"

"You know that, King."

"Yes, of course I know that." Torquas rubbed his bearded cheeks and set the bells to tinkling. The sound irritated Veg Tran beyond measure. "I won't have to take this kind of idiocy much longer, thank the Star," he told himself. He said, "A show of Imperial strength will probably stop any real trouble." Then he added obliquely, "Unless the Order of Navigators is involved."

Torquas was not completely stupefied. "Tran, now listen to me. I want no quarrel with the Navigators. I'll have no trouble with the Theocracy. Why do you think the Navigators are involved?"

"It's too long a story," Veg Tran said curtly. "But there have been indications. Only indications—nothing certain. But it may be necessary to—ah, occupy—a sanctuary. The Navigators' enclave on Aurora."

Torquas's bells rang thinly. "Is that wise, General? I mean, really is that wise?"

"The Gonlani are going to attack Aurora, King. Surely we

are entitled to protect a holy enclave?"

"Well, it seems—" The Galacton's voice trailed off as his half-drugged mind tried to come to grips with the realities of what he was hearing. But Torquas had long ago lost his grip on reality. The statecraft he had been taught as a royal child was lost in a fog of hemp smoke, pinging bells, musical noises, and nonsense poetry. "I mean it seems to me—"

"You need not concern yourself," Veg Tran said. "It is a matter for the General Staff and me to handle. I only want your authority to release thirty Vykan regiments from the city."

Torquas looked alarmed. "Thirty, General? Thirty regiments? That will leave only a handful of Lyri and—"

"And the Vegan Imperials here in the city. That's right." He let his voice turn harsh. "Do you distrust your Vegan troops?"

Torquas shook his head to a tiny clamor of bells. "Don't be offended, General Tran. You Vegans are the most loyal troops in the Empire. I know this. You can be sure of it." Even Torquas recognized the falsity of this statement. Vegan soldiery had been involved in almost every attempt at a coup since the time of Marlana's rebellion. But the worlds of the Vegan Confederacy were among the most populous and powerful in the galaxy. To belabor the truth would be to alienate five hundred million Vegans.

"Well, then, sir." Veg Tran's manner allowed no further discussion. "It is settled then."

Torquas looked helplessly around him at the now empty chamber, garishly illuminated with colored lights. A few years earlier he might have taken this problem to his chaplain, or to any member of the Order of Navigators. But one facet of his faddist life of late had been to boast of his alienation from the religion of his fathers. "You will be careful about the Order, General?" he said. "At least you can promise me that?"

"Naturally," Veg Tran said, standing up. Torquas fumbled in a golden casket for a hemp pipe. The Vegan struck a light on his own torch and held the fire until Torquas was drawing the drugged smoke into his lungs. He stood looking down and half smiling as the King of the Universe's eyes began to film and the handsome face (so like the old images of Glamiss the Conqueror) began to relax into euphoric vapidity.

"Don't concern yourself, Torquas," Veg Tran said evenly, "with anything." He strode swiftly away from his ruler through the soft and cluttered room. At the door he turned and addressed the unseen light-projector operators. "Start the lights," he called scornfully. "The show is about to begin again."

Chapter Ten

What is the Unholy Trinity? The warlock, the Vulk, and science.
      —*The Vulk Protocols*, authorship unknown,
        Interregnal period

In times of social upheaval, a weak king will spawn strong generals whose ambitions, perhaps worthy in themselves, will threaten the stability of the social order. The pattern is immemorial: provincial quarrel, civil war, Imperial intervention—all leading to a suspension of hard-won liberties and eventual tyranny.
      —Varus Milenis, *The New Renaissance*,
        late Second Stellar Empire period

They had left the sea, riding single file up the narrow defile Kynan found, leading to the plateau above. Here the wind from the frozen north was broken by the twists in the land, and the rain fell in curling sheets through the darkness.

Janessa, riding Skua at the rear of the little procession, listened for the sound of the surf. It had grown fainter, though she could still hear the waves rushing up the beach to pound against the foot of the Stoneland cliffs.

The Auroran girl could not imagine how late the hour might

be. It seemed to her that they had been riding for fully half the night, though she knew this was not so. She was wet and cold and perhaps a bit more frightened than she would have Kynan believe. For his part, the Navigator was acting strangely. It was the aftereffects of the Vulk mind-touch, she was certain. He would lead at a pace that was dangerous in the wet darkness, and then from time to time he would slow, almost to walking pace, his white face perplexed and somber, as though unexpected thoughts were emerging from the dimness of memory. Janessa thought of the Vulk Gret and shivered. In the Dark Time, before the forces of Vyka and the Empire had come to Aurora, there had been pogroms on Aurora. The ancient warlords of the planet had encouraged the people to decimate the Vulk community again and again, until now there were nearly none of the strange creatures on Aurora.

The *Protocols* were discredited, of course; but people still said that the Vulk were in some mysterious way beyond human understanding parts of a single great organism. Even today, centuries after the dispersion, they still lamented the destruction of their home world of Vulka—where they were once said to have lived together, sharing thoughts and the Star knew what else, like cells in a great single beast. Scattered over stellar distances, their numbers drastically reduced now, the beast was dead. But the Vulkish mind-powers remained to the survivors. They were everywhere, where one least expected to find them, meddling in human affairs and performing strange rites.

The Rhad thought Auroran anti-Vulkism primitive, but they tolerated it, as men did all over the Empire. It was frightening to Aurorans to see the extent to which the alien beings had infiltrated human society.

Janessa strained to see Kynan's shadowy figure ahead. Even Nav Kynan, a holy Navigator and bond-son of a star king, regularly underwent Triad—and worse. Who could tell what devilment Gret was promoting? Still, she had no choice. It was either this or remain incarcerated at Melissande while her home world took the shock of an attack by the outraged warmen of Gonlan.

The force of the wind increased as they neared the top of the steep draw. Kynan stopped the silver mare and waited for

Baltus and Janessa to come to him.

He leaned forward in the saddle so that he could be heard without shouting and addressed himself to the warlock.

"This is the time, Baltus," he said. "You explain yourself here and now or we put you on foot and let you find your way back to Melissande alone. Why did you come?"

The warlock showed white teeth in his darkly bearded face. "You don't think much of warlocks, Nav Kynan. Few Navigators do. You think us holdovers from the Dark Time." He shrugged his shoulders against the wet cloth of his cloak. "Well, we may be that, of course. But Kreon, the king, was my friend as well as overlord, you know. I served him well for many years. You might remember that now."

"Kreon is dead, Baltus," Kynan said coldly.

"And so will thousands of Aurorans and Gonlani be if Tirzah and LaRoss let Crespus take the warband out."

Baltus's archaic use of the word "warband" for "army" reminded the Navigator just how ancient were the customs of the Rhadan worlds and how far they were now from Algol and the center of the Empire. Serving on the ships of other nations, one easily forgot that the Rim was still populated by men who followed the old ways.

Baltus said, "I don't know what your plan is. I don't even know if it is possible to stop what seems sure to come. But there's a kind of madness at Melissande right now: war fever and the smell of priest-killing. I know that what's planned is just a fuse that will light a great fire if it isn't damped. I see the Empire and the Order mixing in—and the Star only knows what the result of that will be. Nothing good, of that I'm sure."

"What you say seems true enough," Kynan said. "But it doesn't tell me why you are here."

The warlock smiled. "Why are *you* here, Nav Kynan?"

Janessa thought of the Vulk and shivered in the wet cold.

" *'A plan is executed one step at a time,'* " Kynan said. "So it is written." He heard himself and had the belated thought that quoting dogma from the way of the Navigator might make him sound hopelessly stuffy and constrained to Janessa. He wondered why he should care—and could a precept of the beatified Emeric ever be stuffy? Or was it Emeric? Perhaps it was Talvas Hu Chien. He wished he had done better in theology. Then he mentally shook himself and thought that this was no time and place to worry about such priestly things.

The warlock mount muttered impatiently and nipped at Skua, who shook her head and bared her teeth. Janessa murmured to her quietly.

"For what it is worth," Baltus said finally, "I felt I could be of more use to you than to Tirzah or LaRoss. I offer my help." When Kynan made no reply, he went on. "Then, too, remember that I *am* a warlock. You will surely try to take Janessa to the sanctuary on Aurora. The enclave is the only reasonably safe place for her until this madness dies down somewhat. And I would give ten years of my already shortened life to see the sanctuary, Kynan. We are called warlocks —but we are *scientists* . . ." He smiled sadly as both the Navigator and the girl unconsciously made the sign of the Star. "Well, no matter what you think of my calling. I've known you too long to believe you take the old accusations seriously—that we warlocks brought the Dark Time. Yes, it's true the warlocks of the Golden Age made weapons for the kings. Scientists have always made weapons for their rulers— may God and the Star forgive them. It is the way of things. But the Dark Time came because men insisted on fighting among themselves. Across all the sky, they fought and brought ruin on themselves—and on us, their descendants."

This Kynan could not deny. It was history.

"Nav Kynan," the warlock said with feeling, "there is so much to be learned—*re*learned. I believe that warlock and priest must uncover the old knowledge together—" He raised a hand to ward off Kynan's angry denial. "The Order cannot do it alone, Kynan. The priests are too few, the knowledge too broad. Look now—do you realize that four generations after Glamiss the Magnificent reunited the Empire we still don't know what power drives the starships—?"

"That is *holy* knowledge," Janessa exclaimed.

The warlock said firmly, "It is simply knowledge—knowledge that we need, that all men need. Can we of the Second Empire build a starship? The idea is ludicrous—yes, and to you blasphemous, isn't it? But can we? By the Star, we can't even build *aircraft* yet. We are forced to use starships of a million metric tons to transport a bale of goods from Gonlanburg to the other shore of the Gonlan Sea! We can't build a hovercar that will carry us a hundred kilometers without needing to recharge batteries!" He broke off suddenly. "I apologize, Nav Kynan. I feel this so strongly that I risk offending you and your calling. But it is all part of why I am with you—and against men I have known and served most of my adult life. If one warlock can enter a sanctuary of the Order, it is a beginning. I know I run the risk of being burned for heresy and blasphemy—but I don't really believe the Order is so unenlightened now. In Hu Chien's time, yes. But not now."

Kynan regarded the warlock for a long time, listening to the sound of the wind and the rain. Presently he said quietly. "It may be that what you say contains some truth. But there may be war coming. It isn't the time to challege dogma men have lived by since Glamiss's time."

"Let me help you prevent it, Nav Kynan. Perhaps I'll earn my reward in that way."

"I am only a priest, Baltus, not a prince of the Order."

The warlock leaned across the withers of the silver mare and placed his hand over Kynan's. "You are the bond-son of my star king, Nav. That is hope enough for me."

Kynan sat silently for a time and then inclined his head to touch the warlock's knuckles in the ancient Rhad ritual gesture of acceptance of fealty. "So be it, then," he said. "For better or worse, we are bound." Then he spoke softly to the silver mare and led off up the leveling path to the wind-scoured plateau, where lay the path to Gonlanburg.

It was near the hour of dawn when they reached the town, but the stormy darkness was unbroken. The stone houses, most of them roofed with turf, stood shuttered against the weather. The soft pads of the horses' feet made no sound on the wet and muddy cobblestones.

Kynan avoided the watch and skirted the main square of the city, heading the small procession toward the bare field that served the place as a port.

Even at a distance Kynan, Janessa, and the warlock could see the glow of the Lyri starship. The fields of energy surrounding it ionized the raindrops and made them radiate with sympathetic forces.

The intensity of the light and the rate at which it was brightening indicated to Kynan's practiced eye that the great ship was making ready to depart.

Janessa urged Skua forward to ride side by side with the Navigator. "What is it?" she asked.

"Listen," Kynan warned.

The rain rustled on the turfed roofs of Gonlanburg, and in the distance the three fugitives could hear the soft clatter of arms. "LaRoss and Tirzah have sent a detachment to hold the starship," Baltus said softly.

"Brother Evart would never let them aboard," Kynan said.

"True enough. But they can certainly prevent *us* from reaching the ship."

"I don't think Rhad warmen would interfere with me," Kynan said with a confidence he didn't feel.

The air had begun to hum in resonance with the power increase in the ancient engines of the starship. The farther houses were outlined, dark and squat, against the luminosity originating at the port.

Kynan's mare reached the square nearest the field, and now the three of them could see the starship clearly. It was an awe-inspiring sight, even at this distance. The kilometer-long hull pulsed with patterns of light, the magnetic lines of force surrounding the great vessel swirling and changing as the negative charges built up. The nose cone of the control section was fully polarized, so that it looked crystalline, almost invisible, and the control instruments and consoles were dark shapes suspended in space. Kynan could see Brother Evart's cowled figure reclining in the First Pilot's couch and, less distinctly, the outline of Brothers Clement and Pius, the novices who were assisting in the takeoff.

Janessa caught Kynan's mailed arm. "Nav Kynan. Look there—at the edge of the landing ground!"

Kynan had already seen, with sinking heart, the half company of warmen who stood watching the vessel make ready to lift into the night.

That they had come to prevent anyone's taking Janessa aboard the Lyri starship was beyond argument. They were making no effort to delay the departure of the craft. It would have been blasphemous—and impossible, in any case. No force the modern world knew could force entry into a manned starship. But the detachment, some forty men, stood between the watchers and the ship.

Kynan said to Baltus, "Stay here. When I signal to you—come at a gallop."

Janessa protested, "What are you going to do, Kynan? There are too many of them."

"I've no intention of fighting my own people," he said. "But we must reach that ship." He urged his mount forward, and the silver mare's teeth gleamed in the light reflected from the starship. She was making battle sounds and setting Baltus's charger and old Skua to dancing eagerly.

The Navigator rode out of the town shadows at a trot and into the brightness pulsating across the wet grass of the open field. Kynan watched the transparent flank of the control room and prayed to the Star that Brother Evart would be able to see what was happening below him. Everything depended on that. But Evart was such a deliberate man that he might well devote his entire attention to matters within the ship. If this happened, they were lost.

Kynan told the mare to canter now, and she did. He could see the warmen turning to watch him. They had been told to expect more than a single rider, and they were possibly perplexed. He most fervently hoped so.

"You there!" the Rhad officer called. "Is that you, Nav Kynan?"

Kynan did not reply. Instead, he slanted away from the group, angling toward the immense overhanging bulk of the starship's prow.

"Nav Kynan!" the officer called again, mounting his charger. "Stop! We have orders not to harm you—!"

Kynan wheeled the silver mare, at the same moment taking his pistol from his holster. He could look up into the starship's control room, and he cursed Brother Evart with theological precision. The under-priest was paying not the slightest attention to the action developing directly under him on the ground. Kynan could almost hear the intent Navigators beginning to chant the power sequence preparatory to actually lifting the massive vessel from the surface.

The rain stung his face, and he hoped with all his heart that his primitive flintlock had been dried enough by the heat of his body to fire now, when it was needed. The warmen were wheeling and spreading to cut him off.

Kynan raised the clumsy weapon and pulled the trigger. He breathed a prayer of thanksgiving as the pistol fired, spitting sparks and wadding, over the heads of his pursuers. The heavy ball struck the polarized hull of the starship and whined away into the darkness. For a moment the soldiers gaped at the sacrilege. The starships were the holiest things in the known universe. They were the very key to men's survival as a starvoyaging race. To fire a weapon at one, even though it could do the ship no conceivable harm, was a breathtaking sin. And that a Navigator should do it was almost unthinkable.

It was almost so for Kynan himself. With the discharged weapon still in his hand, he muttered an Ave Stella and promised himself severe penance. It would be difficult to find something suitable. He had never committed so unholy an act before. But the situation was desperate, and desperate measures were called for.

He looked up and saw that the sound of the ball striking the hull of the ship had attracted Brother Evart's attention. But Evart was so stolid and unimaginative a man that he merely remained at the control console, staring at the scene below in leaden amazement.

Kynan whirled the silver mare about in an agony of frustration. He shouted furiously at Brother Evart to open the valve, knowing as he did so that, of course, the underpriest could hear nothing of what was being said outside the starship.

"Nav Kynan!" the officer called, galloping nearer. "You must come with us! We want the Auroran girl—"

At this moment Kynan saw with a flash of hope that Evart, within the ship, was rising from the First Pilot's place at the consoles. Had he recognized him on the field below—a Navigator beset by a company of horsemen? What in the Star's name was delaying him?

Kynan turned in the saddle to look at the flank of the ship. A single point of darkness appeared amid the whorls of light. Yes, Evart was dilating the entry valve!

Kynan hurled a command at the silver mare, and she responded with a swiftness that almost unseated him. At an extended gallop, he circled around the line of warmen toward the edge of the field. Kynan signaled to Baltus and Janessa to follow and, without waiting to see if they complied, put his mare directly at the nearest soldier.

The valve was opening, extending a ramp like a dark tongue. The lines of force surrounding the ship shimmered and gleamed. Kynan hoped with all his heart that neither Baltus nor the girl would hesitate. The lights were harmless, but they were ghostly and frightening to laymen.

He shouted, "*Make way, soldier! Make way!*"

The warman, disciplined and trained as most Rhadans, would respond only to his own officer. The silver mare collided with the warman's mount: a thunderous, jarring impact. She was shrieking with savage pleasure, slashing with her tigerish teeth at her rival.

Behind him, Kynan had a momentary impression of thudding pads, and Janessa and the warlock flashed by, heading for the open valve. Kynan saw the Rhad officer's mount go down before Baltus's charge, and then they were past him. He wheeled the mare to follow, but his adversary was too well trained to permit him to escape. The Rhad moved in beside him, still not drawing a weapon. He was a large young man, massive in the arms and shoulders. He threw himself across and carried Kynan to the wet grass.

As they fell, they twisted, and Kynan landed with his weight across his would-be captor. The young warman's breath came out in a whooshing grunt, and he lay stunned. Kynan leaped to his feet and began to run toward the open valve of the starship.

But it was hopeless. On foot he would never make it. The soldiers were closing in on him as he saw the warlock's charger carry him up the ramp and into the ship.

Then he saw Skua, carrying Janessa, pause on the ramp, wheel, and come pounding back toward him. He had no time to protest, no time to do anything but ready himself to catch Janessa's stirrup iron as the old war mare came thundering by. The impact felt as though it would tear his arms from their sockets, but he held on, his feet half dragging, half running. With a great effort he swung himself up on the mare's boney rump and yelled for her to "*Go!*"

Sides heaving with the effort, the ancient animal scrambled

up the retracting ramp and into the diminishing circle of the valve.

The hidden machines sighed behind them, and suddenly the sounds of the rain and the shouts of the frustrated warmen were shut off. Skua stood, head down, flanks heaving, on the floor plates of the entry port.

Janessa and Kynan dismounted and stood, scarcely believing that they were safely aboard, as the humming sound of the ancient engines grew louder and a slight pressure against their feet told them that the starship was lifting, rising into the rainy atmosphere of Gonlan.

Chapter Eleven

Divide and rule.
—Political maxim attributed to Niccolò Machiavelli, Dawn Age philosopher and soldier

—we imagined that the terror of our weapons was such that men would never again seek to settle their differences in warfare. That we were wrong is proved by the civil wars that are now upon us.
—Late Golden Age microfilm fragment found in the ruins of Station One, Astraris, by members of the Astrarian Archeological Foundation, late Second Stellar Empire period

We are being stifled by priests. Let us sever the tentacles of the so-called holy Order of Navigators. Yes, let there be war.
—General the Honorable Alain Veg Tran addressing the Congress of the AbasNav party, middle Second Stellar Empire period

Kynan stood on the deck of the starship's bridge and listened to Brother Evart sing the changing of the watch. The traditional chant, charged with the immense sadness of life in interstellar space, ancient beyond imagining, brought memories of the Theocracy.

In Algol, it took many years for a consecrated religious to learn the way of a Navigator. The office of Spiritual and Temporal Guide of Starships was one so surrounded with ritual, dogma, and ceremony that many a young novice (and Kynan remembered his own doubts) despaired of reaching ordination.

Evart would make a fine Navigator one day, though he must now be suffering nervously under the eye of his superior, as were the other religious in the crew. But all were made uneasy by this radical shift in the ordered progression of events. They had been, until Kynan appeared on the landing ground, in the process of returning the great starship to the Lyran Republic, where it belonged. Now all was changed, and the course was set for Aurora without authority from either the Lyri, who owned the vessel, or from the Theocracy.

Kynan watched the three priests at their consoles and hoped that his own uncertainty didn't show. This was the first time in his young career as First Pilot that he had taken independent action, diverting a starship from its planned schedule. Furthermore, he was a fugitive and possibly an outlaw on his own home world. And he intended to take unconsecrated persons, Janessa and the warlock, into a sanctuary. It was unnerving for an inexperienced Navigator to diverge from the orderly fulfillment of his duties in this way—but he was at a loss to think what else he could do. The situation called for older heads than his, and the sanctuary on Aurora seemed the logical place to find the guidance he needed so desperately.

Meanwhile, Kynan thought, *I am a Navigator, a First Pilot—and I must act like one.* The ghost of a wry smile touched his lips. *Just as though I know what I am doing.*

Being on the bridge of a starship was soothing, however. The soft humming of the walls and hull, the familiar sights and sounds, the sense of *life* that pervaded the great ancient vessel—all helped to build and sustain confidence. With this ship, Kynan thought, I could fly to the end of the sky, to Andromeda and the Magellanic Clouds. It might take a lifetime to reach those distant ports, but the ship could do it.

Austere in clean black clericals, free of his weapon harness, his head covered by the black skullcap of his rank, Kynan stood in command of one of the mightiest engines ever built by the hand of man. It could not help but build confidence, even in one so young.

The viewscreens ahead and behind showed the oddly grouped stars. Those ahead were violet, those behind, red. In the time of Grand Master Emeric, the Mystery of the Red Shift had been the subject of many a learned synod of the Order. Navigators, time out of mind, had pondered its meaning. Now it was known that it was but a natural phenomenon caused by the extreme speed of the ship. Navigator Anselm Styr, an indefatigable investigator (who eventually paid with his life for his scientific curiosity) had discovered that light traveled at a finite and measurable velocity. He had theorized that the Red Shift was caused by the separation of light into its various components when an object—in this case the starship—approached light-speed. (The terms "sublight" and "superlight" had been part of the dogma of star flight since the Dark Time.)

Styr's theory postulated that as a starship accelerated into the faster-than-light speed range, the shift stabilized and the apparent colors of the stars remained unchanged. But the apparent *shape* of the subjective universe was deflected by the increase of the starship's mass to near infinity, causing the star images to group ahead and behind the vessel. He had even suggested that at some point along the velocity curve, the stars would vanish completely and the starship would be ejected from "real" spacetime into a continuum as yet unexplored by men. In this way, the heretic priest had suggested, voyages to other galaxies might be attempted, since the unknown continuum's space-time would probably be of different, and possibly smaller, dimensions than the familiar universe.

Styr's theories were currently discussed in Algol, and as a student Kynan had found them baffling and fascinating. Styr himself, unfortunately, had turned from theoretical to practical physics a century before. He had produced a controlled nuclear reaction, was accused of heresy, and ended his distinguished career on a scaffold at Biblios Brittanis. The Order approached new knowledge—or even the rediscovery of the old—with extreme timidity.

It was the way of things, Kynan told himself. Fear of science was natural among members of a race that had populated the stars only to be brought crashing down into savagery by the hammer blows of the hideous weapons created by their own technology. Rebuilding confidence and civilization after so dark a time as the Interregnum was a delicate business, to be approached with great caution. That, in the end, was the true purpose of the Order of Navigators.

Yet slowly the old mysteries were uncovered. Kynan, like many a young priest before him, dreamed of the time when men would begin to break new ground, rather than redo what the godmen of the First Empire had done before. He hoped this time of discovery would come in his lifetime—but he knew that this was unlikely. He was not even certain that if the time *should* come before his own end, he would fit into the new age, for it would surely be a time when science and religion parted, divided, each discipline going its separate way. *And I am, after all,* he thought, *a priest of the Order Militant.*

One lived one's life in the time allotted by God and the spirit of the Star. Not yesterday and not tomorrow, but today.

He made the sign of the Star and withdrew from the sanctum of the control room, seeking the living spaces and the quarters Evart had assigned to Janessa and Baltus, the warlock.

The journey from Gonlan, at the edge of Rhadan space, to Aurora customarily took from ten to thirty hours, Earth Standard, depending on the relative positions of the astronomical bodies involved. With Brother Evart, Kynan had plotted orbits and trajectories for an intersystem flight of twenty-one hours. Time enough to rest and think and *plan,* for at the moment, he realized with a pang for his own inadequacy, he had no real scheme of action. And in the face of impending war, catastrophe (the Vulk had made *that* very clear), and the Star knew what else, he needed desperately to act wisely and speedily.

For a moment, as he strode through the tunnel-like companionways of the vast, empty ship, he was conscious of his youth and inexperience. *Twenty,* he thought, *is too callow an age to carry the fate of nations.* Still, the Galacton himself was but twenty—and *he* carried on *his* shoulders the responsibility for all the worlds of the Empire. If Torquas the Poet could deal with the problems of two *thousand* planets, surely Kynan the Navigator could deal intelligently with the problems of two.

The warlock was waiting for him in the entryway that led to what must have been, in First Empire times, one of the main troop bays of the ship. The cavernous chamber was sparsely lit: only three small globes of the hundreds in the low overhead burned. The farthest reaches of the bay were lost in shadows.

It was obvious that Baltus had been exploring this section of the craft. His bearded face was set in an expression of delighted wonder familiar to Kynan. Warlocks—as a class—loved the starships and enjoyed nothing more than investigating them without an escort of Navigators, for they were freethinkers, free *researchers,* actually, and the starships were still the most direct link to the wonder-working builders of the legendary First Empire.

"Kynan," the warlock said without preamble. "I have never explored a Lyran starship before. The troop bays are different from the ships of the Rhad."

Kynan stood beside the warlock, looking down the vast empty sweep of the compartment, trying to imagine what it must have looked like filled with the soldiers of the First Empire and their fantastic weapons. "All the starships have differences, Baltus. Each star system—province, actually—supplied troops of a special sort to the armies of the Empire. The Lyri were always infantry. Flying infantry, it appears. Each man was equipped with a device to nullify gravity." He pointed to the oddly honeycombed overhead. "We think the devices were stored in the ceilings when not in use."

The warlock's eyes gleamed hungrily. "What men they were —those ancient ones. By the holy Star, when will the Navigators let us learn from them?"

Kynan said disapprovingly, "The search for old knowledge is the province of the Order, warlock. *Only* the Order."

Baltus shook his head sadly. "No warlock would agree with you there, Nav Kynan."

"Warlocks can still be burned," Kynan cautioned. "Remember that, Baltus."

The older man sighed and shrugged. "But there is so much to know, so much we need to discover."

"The cloister on Algol is the place for that. The cloister and the sanctuaries." Kynan was, after all, a consecrated man and a priest. There were times when he felt as Baltus did—as all warlocks did—that the free investigation of scientific truths was the true heritage of all men, not just priests of the Order. But these doubts were momentary. Man's bloody history bore witness to the dangers of unrestricted science.

Baltus smiled. "We have made *some* progress, Nav Kynan," he said. "In Kier of Rhada's time, you might have handed me over to the Inquisition merely for the suggestion that the Order might be wrong."

Kynan's manner softened, for the warlock and he were old acquaintances. "No, not even in The Rebel's day. The Inquisition was part of the Dark Time. All that is behind us, please God."

Baltus's smile faded. "There will be a dark enough time for Aurora soon, Kynan. What are we to do?"

The Navigator frowned and shook his head. "I wish I knew. My brain is bursting. I don't know which thoughts are mine and which are the Rhadan Vulk's. I keep thinking we must divert and go to Nyor—and yet that can't be right. The danger isn't on Earth. It's here on the Rim. Aurora is the place. The sanctuary, at least." He pressed his fingertips against his skull. "I have been in Triad often enough to know that there should be no conflicts in a man's thoughts afterward. Yet I keep having this urge to turn for Earth. I *know* Gret didn't plant that in my mind. His loyalty is to Rhada. But why—" He broke off, shaking his head in perplexity. "I'm only a starship priest, Baltus. Politics has always baffled me. But why do I keep thinking of Torquas, whom I've never seen? And General Tran—who is like a figure out of a legend to me?"

"When the Vulk implant a man's subconscious, only the Star knows what he may see," the warlock said. "It is told that the Vulk joined with Kier the Rebel to defeat a cyborg in the Three Encounters during Marlana's rebellion, and the star kings swore that he turned to steel during the fight. Who can say what is possible for the Vulk?" He smiled slightly. "Obviously he didn't *remain* steel, since he married Queen Ariane and gave her five children but—" He shrugged. "It is well to turn to steel when one needs to. I think you need to now, Nav Kynan. LaRoss, Tirzah, and General Crespus will be looking for us when the Gonlani army makes a planetfall on Aurora. They'll call us traitors."

"They are my bond-father's men," Kynan said.

"And your bond-father is dead, Kynan. So, for all we know, is Karston the heir. Gonlan is without a legitimate king. LaRoss can rule as he pleases. His loyalty has always been to Karston, but who can tell now—?"

Kynan turned away from the silent, empty bay. "Was I wrong, then? To take Janessa out of Melissande? By all the cybs and little demons, Baltus, could I leave her there as a hostage while our armies level Aurora?"

"Was it your idea?" the warlock asked shrewdly. "Have you asked yourself that? To take her out of Melissande wasn't the act of a fire-breathing citizen of Gonlan—or of Rhada, for that matter."

"The Vulk suggested it," Kynan said, uncertainly. "But—"

The warlock waited, looking closely at the young priest's face.

"No, it was more than the Vulk's suggestion," Kynan said with decision. "It wasn't the act of a loyal Rhad, perhaps. But it *was* what any Navigator would have done. The Order commands a higher loyalty than nationality, Baltus. It must be so, or the Empire would fall to pieces. My bond-father Kreon would have understood. It was Kreon, after all, who gave me to the Order as a child. He was an honorable and religious man. He would say that I have done the right thing."

"Right, perhaps. But dangerous, Nav. Very dangerous. Gonlan without a star king is a peril to all of the Rim. Perhaps more than that. I can't believe all this happened by accident." The warlock spoke earnestly. "There is a pattern, a design—"

"But whose?"

The warlock veiled his eyes, for he knew that what he was about to say would offend the young Navigator. "Only the Empire or the Order make such designs, Kynan."

Janessa awoke from a weary, dozing slumber and lay on her bed listening to the humming of the starship. Like all of the people of the age, she was familiar with the great, ancient vessels that flew between the stars. But the wonder of how this miracle was actually accomplished never failed to fascinate her. From childhood she had kept in her mind the youthful excitement of star travel. That these machines, so incredibly old, could transform the shining lights in the sky into stars and planets where one might walk and live never failed to arouse her sense of the magnificence of her race. Men had built the starships, not gods. That was the glory of it. And perhaps, one day, men might build starships again.

The quarters assigned to her must have belonged, in other times, to the most distinguished personages who star-traveled. The chamber in which she found herself was not immense, but the curving design of the walls and ceilings gave an impression of unlimited space. Mirrored panels reflected her image, and mysterious cabinets with stylized controls filled one entire bulkhead. She had no idea of what those cabinets might once have contained, though she suspected that once there had been hidden machines to store and care for personal belongings of the star traveler using this stateroom.

The bathing accommodations had been partially restored by the Lyri who owned the starship. Water could be made to flow into a sunken, globular depression in the humming deck plates of the small anteroom. But it was obvious that at some time in the distant past, bathing aboard this vessel had been something far more entertaining than a mere immersion of the body in water. Fully a dozen spigots and spray nozzles ringed the bathing globe. Janessa could only guess at their use.

For an Auroran of the middle Second Empire, however, even a hot bath was a luxury, and Janessa wasted no time in taking advantage of it. The uniform of a Rhadan-Gonlani cadet she had worn aboard had been dried and pressed into a semblance of neatness by the junior Navigator on board, and it lay awaiting her when she emerged, refreshed from the bath.

For a moment the Auroran girl stood before one of the shining wall mirrors in her quarters and thought about the magnificent First Empire ladies who must once have seen themselves reflected there. By comparison, she thought ruefully, Janessa of Aurora was a poor thing. Her figure was too boyish by half, she concluded, the result, no doubt, of many hours spent in the warlike training and activities the Rim worlds demanded of their royal women. The unaccustomed brilliance of the electric lights glinted from her smooth, shining hair that curled damply to her shoulders. She stretched and made a face at herself, frowning at the darkening bruises she had acquired on that nightmare flight from Melissande. No First Empire noblewomen had ever been knocked black and blue on horseback in a race across the cliffs of the Stoneland Peninsula, she guessed. She touched the thin scar on her abdomen left by a Navigator surgeon's primitive removal of an inflamed appendix. Surely no great lady of the First Empire had ever been scarred that way, either. Her father's warlock had once told her that Vulks had been the surgeons of the Golden Age and that under proper conditions they operated on humans without leaving a mark on them. Janessa shivered. Perhaps a scar was a small price to pay for not submitting so to the Vulk.

That was senseless prejudice—Kynan would tell her so, she was certain. She turned away from her reflection and began to dress almost angrily. She was most strongly attracted to Nav Kynan, and this, she felt instinctively, was a danger to them both. She was Janessa, heiress to Aurora and betrothed to Karston of Gonlan. A dynastic marriage had been planned while they were still children, and she had never, until now, had cause to question it. And who, after all, she thought with Rim-worlder's arrogance, *was* Nav Kynan? A foundling, an adoptive son of a minor star king. Why, he could have come from anywhere! The good Lord and the Star only knew where the Navigators had found him or why they had placed him in the care of old Kreon, a petty under-king of the Rhad.

Still, she thought with a slow-breaking smile that was suddenly warm with youthful enthusiasm, he was very brave, quite handsome. And she *did* so like the way he looked at her with devotion in his eyes. Janessa of Aurora had seen enough of devotion in the eyes of the young warmen of the rim to know when one of them was falling in love with her.

It was going to cause trouble. There was no doubt of it. But let it! There was already trouble enough brewing. A tiny bit more wouldn't be impossible to bear.

With that, Janessa made her decision. Whatever would be

in this coming war between her country and Kynan's, she *would* have her Navigator if she chose. And choose she did.

Satisfied, she finished dressing and went to seek the young man she had decided to love.

She found him in a bay near the entry valve where they had stabled the horses. He was rubbing the fetlocks of the mare Skua and talking to her in a low voice.

Janessa heard her reply to something Kynan had said with a flick of her gray-maned head. "It was good to fight again," the animal said in that guttural voice of the Rhad warhorse.

Kynan stood and ran a hand over the old mare's neck. "You saved me, you old woman." He laughed softly and added, "And I have stolen you. If we ever return to Gonlan, I must find the money to buy you."

Skua's mind was incapable of developing any interest in the fine points of her ownership. She said, "We fight again soon?"

"I hope not," Kynan said. "Not where we are going."

"It is good to fight," the mare muttered, butting him with her head.

"It is better to live in peace," the Navigator said, more to himself than to the mare, who could never grasp such a concept in any circumstances, bred as she was for battle.

"No," Skua said. "Fight."

Kynan laughed and slapped her flank gently. "Monster," he said.

The mare raised her head at Janessa's approach and bared her tigerish teeth. Janessa said sharply, "Skua!"

The mare shook her head angrily.

"She's jealous of me," Janessa said.

Kynan looked at the girl and replied, "She has reason, lady."

Skua made a threatening noise in her throat, and Kynan rapped her sharply across the muzzle. The mare walked stiffly away, silent on her padded feet. When she reached the place where Baltus's animal lay dozing on the deck, she extended her neck and nipped the sleeping mare's rump. The other scrambled to her feet, outraged.

"They remind me of us," Kynan said. "Quarreling and nipping, always trying to draw blood and never quite knowing why."

Janessa looked at the Navigator's thoughtful face and said, "Of you and me, Kynan? Or Aurora and Gonlan?"

"All of us," the Navigator said. "The Rim worlds and the Inner Planets. The army and the Empire and the Order—*all*. Will there never be peace among us?"

"There has been peace for a century or more," Janessa protested.

"Of a sort," Kynan said.

"There hasn't been a major war between nations of the Empire since Marlana's rebellion in the time of the first Torquas."

Kynan regarded the girl bleakly. "I wouldn't call what happened on Aurora *peace*. It's hard to think of what is going to happen because of it as anything but war."

Janessa looked at Kynan confidently. "But you are going to *prevent* that, Nav Kynan."

Kynan burst into laughter at the girl's bland assurance that he, one man, a minor priest of the Order, could personally hold back the forces that were threatening the peace of the Rim. He put his hands gently on her shoulders and held her. "I shall try, my princess. I shall try very hard," he said.

He would have taken her in his arms and kissed her then, but something began to happen inside his head. He closed his eyes in pain as conflicting images and impulses seemed to lock in combat for control of his will. A shudder swept through him.

"*Kynan, what's wrong?*"

Even the animals sensed his sudden ordeal. They whickered nervously and stamped their pads on the deck.

Behind Kynan's closed eyes, a vast and confused panorama was forming. The Vulk impressions battled with something else, a great, gathering darkness shot through with sudden, unexpected illuminations. Stars and planets whirled in swift, silent motion through an immense void. He seemed to be moving away from the light at terrifying speed. It seemed that time and distance were shrinking, shrinking, until his mind spun in space, deep in the intergalactic night. Around him he could see the luminous spirals of galaxies, like whirlpools of light. And they were *moving*, spinning perceptively, so that the spiral arms pulsed with the life and death of billions upon billions of stars. It was as though the whole of time were being compressed into an instant, so that the *scale* of the universe was being reduced to a fraction of a man's lifetime.

Then he was plunging back toward the light spiral that he knew, somehow, contained that place he called "home." He was falling into a cauldron of light, and the luminosity filled all space, all time. The spinning slowed, and gradually his mind conceived of time again as men had always known it, a flow toward entropy so vast, so deliberate, that a human lifetime was only the quintillionth part of a microsecond in that eternity.

He was humbled, moved beyond his power to comprehend, and he thought of the words "Stellar Empire" in their true context, describing a tiny fragment of the subjective human existence against a backdrop of the vast objective reality of the galaxy.

The Royal Vulk of Rhada seemed to be saying to him: *If you would rule, you should know what it is that you rule— what an insignificant part* of All *men have conquered.*

Kynan was only passively aware that he was crumpled, huddled on the deck, holding his bursting head, hearing Janessa's frightened demands to know what it was that had taken him so suddenly. He thought he sensed Baltus the warlock coming, and Brother Evart, too. They were all frightened for him, he knew that. But the images continued in a roaring torrent through his brain. There were those the Vulk must have given him—but there were others, too, coming from he knew not where . . .

The Vulk's implanted memory seemed to say: *I think I see who you are—may God pity you.*

From somewhere else came the command: *Do not go to Aurora. Go to Earth, to* Earth. *Your destiny lies at Nyor.*

He resisted violently. The sanctuary in Aurora was where his own mind told him he must seek help and guidance. Who could tell whence came these other thoughts? He had never before believed in cybs and demons, but were these strange temptations not very like the temptations put before other religious, in other times, by Antistar, by Evil, by the Devil?

He had an overpowering image of himself seated on a throne that resembled nothing less than the planet Earth, and through his hands—like gems flashing fire—ran the sparkling suns of the Empire. It was purest fantasy. His mind staggered, limped, under the impact of these dreams, and he thought: *I am going mad. Something is destroying me.* He mumbled a prayer to the beatified Emeric: *Intercede for me, kinsman. Intercede for me before the Star throne of God!*

Again came the bombardment, the thrust of greed, an avarice so great it was like gall: *To Nyor, to Nyor, Kynan! Now, do it now!*

No, he thought desperately. *I will not do it! I am a priest of the holy Order Militant. I will do my duty or die in the attempt. Pray for me, beatified Emeric!* His uncontrolled hands tried to form the sign of the Star, and then his bedeviled, abused consciousness refused to accept more, and with Janessa and Baltus staring at him in frightened wonder, Kynan slumped to the deck in exhausted, unnatural sleep.

Chapter Twelve

Though denied by ecclesiastical historians (such as the redoubtable chronicler of the middle Second Stellar Empire period, Bishop Julianus Mullerium), it is an irrefutable fact that by the final years of the Torquan Age, the Order of Navigators had far exceeded its original raison d'être: the guardianship of the First Empire's interstellar vessels. Navigator-astrophysicists studied stellar mechanics, Navigator-surgeons practiced in all but the most primitive nations, Navigator-engineers probed the mysteries of interstellar engine design and ship construction, and Navigator-physicists gingerly examined the atom in sanctuaries scattered about the inhabited galaxy. Nor were the arcane disciplines ignored by the priestly researchers. Psychiatry, psychometry, psionic factors, and psycho-control of personality were all considered by Navigators. Areas of investigation denied as "heretical" or "sinful" to the commonality were at the same moment in time probed by carefully selected members of the Order in secret. No apologist for the Order has ever been able to justify to modern historians this basic hypocrisy . . .
—Varus Milenis, *The New Renaissance*,
late Second Stellar Empire period

* * *

If the mountain will not come to Mohammed, Mohammed must go the mountain.

—Dawn Age proverb

The starship of the Five hung in space just out of detector range of the Lyri vessel commandeered by Kynan for the flight to Aurora. The heads of the Order's intelligence apparatus were locked in argument and disputation. The discussion, tense to begin with, had been precipitated into near vituperation by the Tactician's flat assertion that both the Psychologist and the Technician had failed miserably in their assigned tasks. Tasks, the soldierly Tactician declared with great heat, that were essential to the completion of the Order's most secret and cherished plan.

The Logician, more anonymous than the others in his heavy black cowl, said placatingly, "Recriminations aren't likely to be useful at this point." He addressed himself to the Technician in tones of irritating rationality. "You are quite certain there has been no malfunction in the equipment?"

"I'm trying to explain it to you, if I may be permitted," the Technician said testily. A lifetime spent with electronic and psionic circuits left him with little patience for human refusal to accept obvious facts. "Our contract with him has been failing ever since that cursed Vulk mind-touched him. I had no idea a single Vulk could have such an effect. It has always required two plus a human for a complete Triad. And even then, I have never gotten a response like this one."

"A *lack* of response, wouldn't you say?" The Tactician said.

The Technician shrugged. "The equipment is functioning perfectly. The cortical implants are agitating the receptors with a full-signal strength. But the Vulk introduced a confusion factor. I don't know how else to put it. The failure is psychological. I'm sure of it. He should have been conditioned to resist the mind-touch—"

The Psychologist objected. "That would have been impossible and you know it. Furthermore, there was no reason to attempt any such resistance. Priests of his rank undergo Triad at least twice a year. What would the result have been? He would have been cloistered—or deep probed by the Vulks of the College of Religious, and the whole plan surfaced."

"I always felt the plan was sacrilegious," the Theologian said heavily. "It is the hand of the Star."

"Nothing of the sort," the Logician said thoughtfully. "Simply an unpredictable factor. No one could have guessed Gret's power—and no one could have guessed that the boy would even *meet* the Rhadan Vulk. It was Kreon, after all, who was supposed to supply the surface stimuli to get him to Nyor. The point is, what now?"

A heavy silence fell on the five Navigators. The images still flickered on their consoles. A miniature Janessa and a tiny Baltus carried a manikin Kynan through what seemed to be the passages of a starship. But the holographs were distorted, indistinct.

"Can you apply more power?" the Tactician asked gruffly.

"I'm very nearly off scale now," replied the Technician. "I couldn't have penetrated his consciousness at all if it hadn't been for the resonance of the locator planted in the girl."

The Psychologist said, "He couldn't take a deeper penetration in any case. You saw what the conflict did to him. The Vulk's implants sent him quite literally out of the universe, and all we did was drive him half mad." He retracted his cowl, baring a narrow, pale face and deeply set dark eyes that glinted in the greenish glow of the holographs. "He *wants* to go to Nyor. He doesn't know why, and that's the problem. What's happening there? Is there anything on the receiver?"

"Transmission at this distance is spotty," the Technician said. "But our transsender has picked up the ionization trails of five starships going into trans-stellar flight. It is almost certainly General Veg Tran's expedition to Aurora. The Gonlani strike force is embarking now, and they could reach Aurora within twenty hours or less. The time is now. There is no doubt of it. To reach Torquas with Tran away is exactly what we hoped for. A perfect check."

"Except that we can't move our most important piece," the Logician said dryly. "The Vulk seems to have forestalled us."

"The damned Vulks," the military Tactician said angrily. "Wherever you look—wherever you turn over a rock—there they are."

"Ah," the Psychologist murmured. "Straight from the *Protocols*, that. Fascinating xenophobic syndrome."

The Tactician glared at his colleague but he did not reply.

The Technician returned to a close scrutiny of his instruments. "The warlock and the girl have put him to bed in one of the passenger cells."

"Those ancient Lyri loved luxury, that's certain," the Psychologist said, studying the visible appointments of the Lyri starship's interior.

"Interesting, but hardly useful or pertinent," the Tactician said.

"I disagree," the Psychologist said. "If they will leave him alone, in those surroundings—it is just possible I may be able to trigger the action response our electronic friend here has been unable to elicit."

The Tactician folded his arms across his massive chest to prevent the trembling of his hands. He did not want the others to see how agitated he had become. "Time is vital. Can you do it quickly?"

The Psychologist shrugged. "Quickly as may be. He must sleep first. Fortunately, we've put him through such a hell in the last few moments that he must be exhausted."

"In twenty hours LaRoss, Tirzah, and Crespus will have their troops on Aurora," the Tactician said. "Tirzah and Crespus are idiots. They're simply puffed up with Rim-world arrogance and want revenge. But LaRoss is no fool. I'd wage my life on his being Alain Veg Tran's man."

"Impossible," murmured the Theologian.

"Not impossible, Preacher. Not impossible at all. Those priest-killers who attacked the boy on the way to Melissande were LaRoss's bullies. You may be sure of it."

"I agree," said the Logician.

"Karston, the heir to Gonlan, is another fool. And an arrogant one, to boot. If he ruled in Gonlan, LaRoss would surely have the power," the military man continued. "And Alberic of Rhada is old. Who is to say LaRoss isn't thinking of a coup that could take over the whole of the Rhadan Palatinate? Please note that he has not yet let the Vulk leave the planet."

The Logician nodded approval. "A reasoned exposition of

the situation. Better than one might normally expect from a soldier."

The Tactician glared at him from beneath his cowl.

The Technician interrupted. "Even assuming that we can move the boy to Nyor, Gonlani troops will be near the sanctuary within hours after they make their planetfall. We can expect the Aurorans to delay them for perhaps a day—"

The Theologian spoke. "But won't the Gonlani attack Star Field first? Why should they desecrate a sanctuary?"

The Logician shook his head. "Sorry, but that is exactly what they will do if LaRoss leads them—and he will, of course. I think we must all agree now that LaRoss is acting for Veg Tran and the AbasNavs. There's not much doubt that it was Tran's men who attacked the celebration at Star Field in the first place. Tran *wants* to intervene in a Rim-world squabble—but it must be at the sanctuary."

"His Navigators will never permit it," the Theologian declared.

"His Navigators will do what Navigators have always done, old one," the Tactician said brusquely. "They'll pilot his ships and land his men where he wants them landed. Their crisis of conscience won't come until after they've done that. And then it will be too late. You'd do well to remember that we are not a *nation,* Father, but an Order. The Theocracy serves *all* the states of the Empire—"

"The Order serves God and the holy Star," the Preacher said with emotion.

The Tactician grunted. "Perhaps I've grown too worldly for a priest. But someone once said that God is always on the side of the strongest battalions. Veg Tran will raid the sanctuary because somehow he has discovered that we have been doing nuclear research there—"

The Theologian's eyes brimmed with tears. "It is the will of God, then. I have never believed that the Order should tamper with such sinfulness—"

"Amen to you," the Logician murmured, "but it is rather late to think of that. Tran imagines he can obtain energy weapons from the Auroran sanctuary—and it is just possible that he actually can." He turned an inquisitive eye toward the Technician, who looked away and busied himself with adjustments of his machines. "Well, no matter. Only the Galacton can stop him if he tries to arm himself with nuclear bombs. And we all know what our poet-king is. That is why Kynan *must* reach Nyor without delay." He looked around him at his companions. "Are we agreed on that?"

The cowled priests nodded.

"Then do what you must," he said to the Psychologist. He stood and moved away from the glowing consoles. "For myself, I have been at these machines too long. I must rest."

The Theologian, too, stood. He moved with difficulty, as though age and weariness had invaded his fragile body. "We would do well to leave our colleague here—" He inclined his head toward the Psychologist. "While we pray for his success and for the safety of our Order. Will you all come to the chapel with me?"

The Technician and the Tactician rose to their feet uncertainly. But their manner became more assured as the Theologian made the sign of the Star over them. One by one they glided from the room after him, for though they were indeed worldly men (their duties demanded it), they were also priests, convinced that *en fin* it was God's work they were about.

The Psychologist watched them go and then turned to the instruments reaching across the fluid hyperspatial void toward the Lyran starship, where lay Kynan of Gonlan, Navigator, and in this age (the Psychologist assured himself) the most important person in the galaxy.

Chapter Thirteen

In the dimness of the Dawn Age, that mystical time before man left the surface of his home planet, we may still see darkly the specter of conflicts that arose between Church and State. Empires beyond counting have fallen because the community of religious and the power structure of the nations failed to understand that they should make common cause against the powers of the hostile and unfeeling universe.
— Emeric of Rhada, Grand Master of Navigators, early Second Empire period

The priests of the Order rode at my side and brought the blessing of God and the Star to Vykan arms. Thus did I conquer.
— Glamiss of Vyka, First Galacton of the Second Stellar Empire

Has this happened before? Must this happen again?
— Final recorded words of Rigell XXVIII, last Galacton of the First Stellar Empire, at the sack of Nyor (circa 4,000 GE)

Torquas the Poet stood on the deck of the Imperial barge

and looked across the smooth water of the East River toward the towers and spires of his capital. In the morning sunlight the roofs of Nyor, golden, silvered, some patterned with gardens and white columns, all gleamed like the scattered contents of some fairy treasury. From this distance, and framed by green water and a cornflower blue sky, Nyor was beautiful. She fit her description of Mistress of the Skies.

Behind him, a group of black-skinned Altairi flautists were playing a softly dissonant melody; over the sound of the music he could hear the chatter and laughter of the gilded young nobles of the court. Sebastian, the slender adolescent cyborg from the Polarian Confederacy, was dancing on the teakwood deck. Torquas could hear the sibilant rustle of his golden mail and the pinging tone of the finger cymbals tapping out the love rhythms of the strange planets that had given him birth. Florian, the heiress of Bellatrix, was laughing and telling a languid group of courtiers of some adventure among the Rim worlders. Torquas caught a single phrase: "—beautiful men, but too fierce, too angry. They weary one so—"

The Galacton moved his sandaled feet on the deck and let the flower he was holding fall into the green waters of the river. He watched the tiny splash and the ripples that lapped against the hull of the great barge and were gone. Florian was right, of course, about the Rim worlders. Only the Rim troubled the tranquility of the Empire. He drew a deep breath and looked across the water toward the southern tip of Tel-Manhat. A squadron of starships hovered there, meters above the rocky shingle of beach, their boarding nets aswarm with warmen in full fighting kit. Veg Tran was embarking the last formations of the peacekeeping force for departure to the Aurori sector.

Torquas shook his head half in anger. The bells in his hair and beard tinkled musically, but their sound quite failed to please him. He saw something else that failed to please him, as well. It was a military cutter setting out from the south shore, oars flashing in the sunlight, and General Veg Tran's personal standard flapping languidly at the stern. Tran coming to take his leave, no doubt. Torquas frowned and looked away. He wished the man would simply go and have done with it. The

Vegan always managed to make Torquas feel the fool and quite inadequate, somehow.

Why was it, Torquas wondered, that he could do this? And why was it that he, Torquas the Galacton—the veritable King of the known universe—should always feel it prudent to do exactly as the dreadful man said? For Tran's sake, Torquas had reduced the number of Navigators at court to a bare minimum. There had been bitter words with the Grand Master ben Yamasaki over it. And though the Star knew that certainly Torquas didn't actually *believe* in all that rot the Navigators preached, the people of the Empire *did,* and so Tran and his AbasNav bullies getting their way was all very well, but who had to pay for it? Torquas, *that* was who paid. By the veritable Star, Tran was as troublesome to the Empire as the whole of the Rim—but without him what could be done? My ancestors conquered the sky, Torquas thought bleakly, and ruled an Empire—but I am not as they were. He felt weak and without purpose. There were actually times, when he found himself surrounded by the nihilistic hedonists he had gathered to be his court, that he felt as though he were acting a part: the simpering young aristocrat with perfumed beard and bells in his hair. By the spirit of blackest space, how his fighting ancestors would have laughed at the spectacle of Torquas, Galacton, Commander of the Starfleets, Defender of the Faith, and Hereditary Warleader of Vyka!

But it was so much easier to be the Sybarite while men like General Veg Tran ran the Empire. *Sloth consumes me,* he thought. Was there the beginnings of a poem there? Perhaps an epic, to sing the end of a noble, savage line of star kings. Torquas, thirteenth of that name. Torquas the Last.

He moved his head again, and the sound of the platinum bells irritated him. He snatched them from his shoulder-length hiar and threw them into the water. They sank without trace. So will the Torquans go, he thought, and self-pitying tears came into his eyes. Out of Vyka came Glamiss Magnifico and his sons: the warrior kings who brought mankind out of the Black Time. And now—was it really over? Did the end of the line lie just beyond the horizon? Did the Second Stellar Empire belong now to the Veg Trans?

The Galacton watched the approaching cutter. The water sparkled at its raked prow: a froth of diamonds. The sunlight glinted from the steel scales of the mailed warmen at the gunwales. And Sebastian, the Polari cyborg, danced nearby and brushed the Galacton's bare skin with the edge of a cymbal. Torquas jerked his shoulder away in annoyance, and the courtiers tittered with languid laughter.

The sunshine was bright, almost metallic. It hurt Torquas's eyes. He really felt rather unwell. Last night's drugs had left a residue in his throat. This morning he had forbidden his companions to smoke hemp on the barge, but it was obvious that some had defied him, for the tang of the stuff was already in the air. *They don't even obey me,* Torquas thought petulantly. *I am their King, and they don't even obey me when I tell them a simple thing like "No drugs on the barge this morning because I'm ill."* What sort of loyalty was that?

The cutter was curving in across the calm water, making ready to come alongside the Imperial barge. Torquas could hear the rattle of shipping oars and the quiet, clipped commands to the warmen and crew. He could see Veg Tran in the stern: he wore ceremonial mail and a black surcoat with the golden flail and grain-sheaf insignia of Vega embroidered on it. The Veg family crest. One would think that an Imperial general starting a peace-keeping expedition to the Rim would at least wear the sunburst of the Empire. If it were Glamiss he were reporting to, or even any one of the noble Vykes who had once ruled in Nyor, he would certainly not have dared such arrogance. *But it is Torquas the Poet who rules here,* the young man thought bleakly. *Anything goes.*

The general's face was stern under the rim of his helmet. Torquas met the older man's eyes across the water and turned away. He wished there were a Navigator here now. Somehow, a priest at his side would have made this encounter more bearable. But there were no longer Navigators at court. Only the priests actually in command of the starships had a place, now that Tran's AbasNav bullies were everywhere. And there were even sacrilegious rumors that the Vegan was, in fact, training unconsecrated men to pilot the holy vessels. A shiver of superstitious dread ran down Torquas's back. He considered himself completely liberated from the old religious views, of course, but the thought of secular men actually piloting starships churned the darkness in some pit of racial memory. It was quite out of the question, really. Tran, no matter how he hated the clergy, would never dare drive the Navigators from the sacred starships. But a lingering doubt remained, like a bead of undigested horror deep inside him, under the heart.

It was too much to think about—too painful to contemplate.

The Lady Florian joined him at the rail. Her silver headdress, a tall filigree crusted with gem stones, flashed in the sunlight. She wore the low-hanging skirt, wasp-waisted and gathered at her ankles, that she had popularized among the women of the court. From her hips to her chin she wore only a complex trellis of vines and flowers painted on her naked skin. A cloying sweetness of scent from southern Africasia surrounded her. She was really quite beautiful, Torquas thought disinterestedly. But ornate. Intricately clothed, made-up, *worked*. Like a poem that might have once been lovely but that had been unwritten, edited, rewritten again and still again, until all spontaneity and life was gone from it. Florian, at twenty, was encased in artifice. There was no way of knowing what sort of *person* there was under the appliqué—or even if there was a *person* there at all.

"Who is that with Tran?" she asked.

Torquas noted now that Tran wasn't alone in the stern of the cutter. There was a young warman with him, a Rhad by his harness. The proud, pale face was like carved ivory in the morning light.

"I heard that Tran had a guest at Saclara," Forian said speculatively. "A Gonlani-Rhad. Some sort of barbarian princeling." It had become fashionable among the nobles of the court to call citizens of the outlying sectors of the Empire "barbarians." Florian was *always* fashionable. "He's very handsome, isn't he?"

Torquas studied the cold, set face of the Rhad. He remembered now, too, that there had been talk of a Gonlani warman at Saclara. Karston, that was the name. Son of the star king of Gonlan, who was a dependent of old Alberic of Rhada. What was Tran doing bringing him here? And why was he taking him on a straightforward peace-keeping campaign on the Rim? It was never wise for the Empire to take sides in the petty dynastic squabbles of the subject nations. That much of statecraft Torquas remembered from the endless sessions with his warlock and Navigator tutors in childhood. He frowned with an effort to remember. That first evening Tran had mentioned the need to take troops to the Rim he had said—what? The Vegan had burst in on a two-day hemp-gathering, and it was difficult to remember exactly what was said now.

The cutter touched the side of the barge, and the crewmen were making her fast. Florian was eying the "barbarian" with distinct interest.

Torquas knit his brows with the effort to recall Tran's exact words. Something about protecting a Navigator's sanctuary from the Gonlani. Tran—showing concern for the clergy. He most certainly should have questioned that. But there had been the drugs and the music, and somehow it hadn't seemed inconsistent.

"The Gonlani are going to attack Aurora, King. Surely we are entitled to protect a holy enclave?" That was it. Those had been Tran's exact words. And now here he was with a Gonlani-Rhad prince—and over there, across a few meters of open water, a squadron of starships was embarking Tran's own Vegan division and thirty regiments of Vyk soldiers. What was going *on* here? How could something like this happen—and what did it mean?

Suddenly, the Galacton began to grow afraid.

For his part, Karston of Gonlan was uncertain of his own status among these glittering Imperials. General Veg Tran had shown him considerable hospitality, first at his Saclara estates, and later here in Nyor. Karston had been entertained with wild-dog hunts in the Saclara Valley and with military ceremonials in the capital. But he was never without an armed escort of Tran's personal troops, and until now, only moments before embarkation of the expeditionary force, he had not been allowed to call upon the Galacton as was his hereditary right as a star king of the Empire.

It was characteristic of Karston that he resented the implied slight on his noble rank more than the unquestioned loss of his liberty and freedom of action. Tran frightened him, though he would have let himself be cut to bits before admitting it. And though his outward poise remained intact, he was badly shaken by the interview with Tran on the terrace at Saclara. To a man of his age, the very existence of the legendary energy weapons of the First Empire was anathema. For many generations the people of the nation-state created by Glamiss the Magnificent and his captains had been nurtured on the concept of freedom from the world-smashing death that had ended the Golden Age. Now Tran, through the instrument of Karston's own treachery to his king and father, reached to take such weapons in hand once more.

Karston stood now at his place in the cutter as the craft was made fast to the Imperial barge. In spite of his misgivings, he could not help but be impressed by the affluence and splendor all around him. The barge was a broad-beamed ship, blunt at bow and stern, and driven by captives turning massive twin screws deep below the waterline. The hull was silvered so that it blazed like newly minted coins in the bright sunshine. The Imperial pavilion occupied most of the sterncastle: a silken replica of the complex tents of the herdsmen of Vyka. Pennons trailed almost to the waterline from the spiked staffs around the gunwales. On each was embroidered the insignia of one of the Galacton's private holdings: the hammer and ax of Vyka, the reaper of Antares, the crown and arrow of Sirius, and fully a dozen others. The descendants of that first tribal chieftain of Vyka who had looked to the stars had done very well, indeed. Their personal wealth, Karston thought greedily, must be almost beyond tally.

The ship, a full two hundred meters from stem to stern, moved sluggishly in the slow swell that invaded the river from the Eastern Sea. A guard of honor, Vyks and Vegans by their harness, had formed at the gangway that had been lowered to the deck of Tran's cutter.

A few disinterested faces lined the polished railing. Apparently most of the young courtiers of Torquas's entourage did not think a visit from a departing general worthy of much interest. Karston could hear the sound of laughter and music on deck, and the tinging noise of cymbals.

He felt gauche and ill-dressed in his warman's harness, even though he had taken pains to wear the feathered cape of a Rim-world star king. He was aware of the fact that he was not yet, technically, at least, entitled to such finery. Nor would he be until the council of Gonlan informed him that he was, in fact, star king of the Gonlani-Rhad. And even then, his title needed to be confirmed by old Alberic of Rhada.

Early the previous evening, he had watched from the high terraces of Tran's quarters in the city as five starships carrying the first elements of Vegan warmen departed the city for Aurora. At least, Tran had said Aurora was their destination; but it seemed quite likely to Karston, after two weeks of Tran's suppressive "hospitality," that the Vegans were bound for Gonlan. A division of Vegans and thirty regiments of Vyk Imperials seemed far too powerful a force for the task of peace-keeping on Aurora, while a Veg division—properly deployed—could very easily hold Gonlan after the departure of most of the Gonlani-Rhad troops for Aurora.

Karston felt an unwilling admiration for Veg Tran in this situation. He was wagering everything on one bold evolution: to hold Gonlan as a base, to interpose himself between the Aurorans and the Gonlani-Rhad and violate an enclave of the Order to obtain the ultimate weapons. If all his moves succeeded, and there was no reason to suppose that they would fail now, this gilded gathering of popinjay courtiers floating on the sunlit waters of the East River would very soon be bowing to a new, *de facto* Galacton.

Tran was stepping on board the barge now, and Karston followed him. There was a stir among the limpid courtiers as a young man in ornate harness came forward. Karston had an impression at first only of elaborately curled hair and beard and almond-shaped blue eyes outlined in cobalt make-up. A golden circlet bearing the Imperial sunburst of the Empire gleamed in the morning brightness.

This, then, was Torquas the Poet. Portraiture had never reached a high degree of perfection in the Second Empire, and the ancient science of "photography" remained one of the lesser mysteries. Thus it was that the only likeness of the Galacton Karston of Gonlan had ever seen was the relief profile of the Vyk face etched into the Imperial coinage.

Tran was addressing the young ruler in military, almost brusque tones. He used the familiar Vegan title of "Leader" rather than the more formal "King." This in itself was a measure of his contempt for the present head of the House of Vyka.

The women of the Galacton's group had gathered, and more than a few of them were eying Karston's massive physique with interest. And Karston, young and a Rhad, had let his attention be diverted from the face and figure of the richly caparisoned Vyk, to whom Tran was presenting him.

Karston now gave his attention to the proprieties and drew himself up to salute the ruler of the Second Empire.

His mouth dropped open, and the blood drained from his face. He felt the impact of an impossible, improbable shock in his knees and elbows. For one ghastly moment he thought he might actually stumble and fall.

He was looking into the face of his bond-brother Kynan. Kynan the Navigator. The *priest*. Kynan the *foundling*—

He fought back an impulse to cry out, to deny the evidence of his own eyes. What he saw, what stood there before him, was blatantly, *obviously* impossible. Yet it was so. Kynan. *Kynan* to the *life*.

The young Galacton was regarding him with an expression of languid perplexity, a half smile on his made-up lips.

Karston took a firmer grip on himself and made an unbelieving obeisance. He glanced at General Tran, but the older man showed no expression other than one of impatient contempt. He thought, Karston realized with great clarity, that meeting the ruler of the known galaxy was overpowering a simple Rim-worlder's breeding and manners. *He didn't know*—

"I am sorry you haven't had time to sample the enjoyments of our court, Karston of Gonlan. Perhaps on your return you'll join us here in Nyor—" The Galacton was speaking, making the sort of polite conversation one might expect from a great king to one of his lesser nobles. Karston studied the astonishingly familiar face. Identical. But for the long hair and the perfumed beard and the painted eyes and mouth, it was his bond-brother Kynan who stood before him. There could be no mistake.

Kynan, he thought, shaken—twin brother to Torquas, Galacton, descendant of royal Vyks—heir to mighty Glamiss himself. It was staggering, dismaying—but there could be no other explanation.

Karston was dynast enough to know what a disaster for a royal house the birth of twin sons could be. For the most royal house of all, such an event could be catastrophic: raising the specter of wars of the succession, civil strife with each faction claiming a royal prince as their own and legitimate heir to the Imperium.

What better solution, then, to choose one son to bear the name and titles and to spirit the other away to the end of the sky to be raised in harmless obscurity?

But who could have been entrusted with such a task?

Who could have the power to take a newborn from a royal queen and deliver him, in time, to the house of a petty noble on the rim of the known world—and thence to Algol Two, to the cowled men of the Theocracy?

Only the Navigators. Only they—

With a sudden insight that was like a revelation, Karston realized that he possessed information worth infinitely more than the overlordship of the Gonlani-Rhad.

What he had this moment discovered was something that could truly shake the Trans and Torquases and Grand Masters, could shake the very foundations of the Empire—

He wondered if Kynan knew, and the answer came swiftly and surely. Kynan had no inkling of his origins. Kynan was a priest, a Navigator, nothing more, a man content to spend his life piloting starships and spreading the faith of the Star amid the heathen.

Standing on the deck of the Imperial barge, face to face with the ruler of his world, Karston of Gonlan had to suppress the wild impulse to shout with laughter.

General Veg Tran was regarding him speculatively. Oh, no, Tran, Karston thought. *Perhaps you may be allowed to know, but only when—* and *if—it profits me, Karston, star king of the Gonlani-Rhad.* And now, who could say how much more?

The formal meeting was swiftly concluded, and Karston, hardly remembering how or what he said, took his leave of Torquas and his court. As he returned to the cutter and watched Tran in final, whispered consultations with the

Galacton, Karston had difficulty containing his excitement. He looked across the water to the starships. The embarkation of Vyk troops was nearly complete. Only moments ago he, Karston, had come across the waters of the river downcast and half frightened of the forces to which he had committed his fortunes.

Now, oh *now*, the game looked far, far more appealing. *I thank you, dear brother,* he thought savagely. *I thank you, wherever you are.*

When Kynan opened his eyes, he saw Janessa, her head haloed by the glowing light in the overhead. Behind her, the Navigator could see the concerned face of Baltus the warlock. Somewhere in the compartment, Brother Evart crouched in the shadows; Kynan could hear him reciting the Prayer for Absolution.

Kynan spoke with difficulty. "I'm not dead yet, Evart," he said.

The junior priest was upon him in an instant, all shining eyes and flapping black clericals. *"Gloria! Gloria stella!* Emeric has interceded! Praise God! We were helpless, Nav!" Evart exclaimed tremulously. "We had no idea what sickness had struck you down—"

Kynan closed his eyes to ease the throbbing ache in his head. He felt Janessa touch his brow with a cool hand.

"Where are we now, Evart?" he asked.

"We have just sung the position, Nav Kynan. We are four hours from planetfall."

Kynan nodded wearily. "Go back to your post. I will be on the bridge before it is time to orbit."

"Yes, Nav Kynan, I'll do as you command." Evart gathered himself and moved to the doorway. Standing at the scuttle, he turned and said, "The novices will offer ten *Aves* and a *Pater* for your recovery, Nav."

"My thanks," Kynan said patiently. "Now stay at your post, brother."

The junior priest made an expansive sign of the Star and murmured, *"Mea culpa,* First Pilot."

Weak as he was, Kynan winced at the breach of protocol. A Navigator was never called "First Pilot" before unconsecrated persons. But in Evart's nervous state, such fumbles should probably be forgiven.

The warlock came forward and studied the Navigator's pale face. "I've never seen anyone taken as you were, Nav Kynan. Has anything like this ever happened before?"

Kynan shook his head on the pillow.

"It must be the effects of the Vulk's mind-touch. Perhaps it is hazardous without a complete Triad."

Kynan essayed a smile. The warlock was like all of his kind —a questioner. "It was written by Talvas the Inquisitor, Baltus—'Seek not *why*, or *how*.' "

The warlock smiled back at the priest in silent conspiracy. "That was long ago, Nav Kynan. You don't believe it any more than I do."

Kynan tried to frown. "Take your heresies out of here. I'm well enough now."

The warlock said, "I'll go comfort that old witch of a mare. She almost clawed us when we took you from the stable." He inclined his head in polite withdrawal. "But we'll still have to find out what caused your attack, won't we? It could happen again—under more trying circumstances. I'll leave you with that thought."

That thought, in fact, had been troubling Kynan more than he would have cared to say. Suppose he was stricken while piloting the starship? Or before the seniors of the sanctuary? What then? Almost without volition, his hand tightened on Janessa's.

"I was frightened, Kynan," she said softly.

"And so was I," he said candidly. "I still am."

"Was it because of the mind-touch?"

"I don't know. It seemed more than that. As though there were something *here* inside my head." He pressed his fingers into his dark, cropped hair. He drew a shuddering breath. "Dreams, Janessa. *Such* dreams—" He despaired of ever being able to express to anyone the wild visions he had experienced. "I was a king—no, *the* king. And I saw—the universe —everything—all of space and time. Galaxies were like toys—" He broke off because the frightened expression on the girl's face told him that his words were poor things to tell of what he had dreamed. He could only say, "I think one day we shall find that things are not as we believe them to be. I had a glimpse of that." How could he express to her the insane urge to turn the ship and strike out across the empty parsecs for the galaxy's middle marches and Earth? What possible reason could he give for such a wild notion when there was none? Could *be* none?

"Kynan," the girl said with surprising understanding, "you are deeply troubled now."

"I am, Janessa." The Navigator frowned. "I don't know how to express it well—but it is as though I am not my own master any longer." He broke off because that didn't say exactly what he wanted to convey to Janessa. "I have been a Navigator and before that a junior and a novice. In one way, I've *never* been my own master. I have always served the Order and the Empire. But I have always been a free man, a Navigator, and a citizen of the Empire—in that order. Now, somehow, I no longer feel free—" He shook his head in exasperation. "How can I make you understand something I don't understand myself."

"Perhaps I do understand," Janessa said, "a little. We are all like chips caught in a current. Something is moving us along, and we don't really know what it is. I feel that, too."

He smiled at the girl. He had misjudged her intelligence and sensitivity, that was plain. "I have this insane notion that we should be going to Earth and not to Aurora at all. Can you understand that?"

"No. But if it is what you think we must do, then we shall do it."

Kynan shook his head. "That's part of what I mean. *I* know —the part of me that is *me*—knows that we must stop LaRoss and Crespus before they attack your people. This other thing *here*"—he pressed his forehead again—"is what plagues me with dreams of going to Earth and being a king—" He stopped, aghast at what he had put into words. "There, you see? By the holy Star, I think I may be going mad!" What he did *not* say was that the impulse was strongest when Janessa was near him. Insanity.

Janessa said slowly, carefully, "And be a *king,* Kynan?"

"I tell you I must be losing my mind. That's evidence enough, isn't it?"

"It is the Vulk that's put such ideas into your head," Janessa said with feeling.

Kynan shook his head.

"They're wicked creatures, Kynan. All people know that."

"All *Aurorans* know it," he said. "And they are wrong." His tone permitted no argument, and the girl remained silent, chastised for her racial prejudice. "We are all children of God, Janessa," he said to her sternly, very much the clergyman now.

"Yes, Nav Kynan," she said humbly.

"I don't expect you to believe that all at once. But you will." He tightened his grip upon her blunt, strong hand. "Will you not?"

Janessa looked at him with shining eyes. "For you, Kynan," she said boldly.

Kynan drew a deep breath and closed his eyes. His head still pained him, and there was a throbbing insistence behind his eyes.

"Shall we go to Earth, then?" the girl asked. "It is for you to say."

Kynan's longing was like hunger, like thirst. Earth. Nyor. The Mistress of the Skies. He shook his head and said, "We stay on course for Aurora."

A silent voice seemed to shriek in his skull: *To Nyor, King, to Nyor—!*

Janessa's eyes widened with new fear as she saw the sweat beading the Navigator's forehead. "Aurora," he said again.

Kynan managed a grim smile of victory, for it *was* a victory, of some kind, over some*thing,* though he knew not what. He forced himself to think very clearly and slowly: *Whoever you are, whatever you are—you've lost. I am still a free man.*

Chapter Fourteen

There is no such thing as absolute defeat or victory. There are only degrees of success or failure.
—Glamiss of Vyka, early Second
Stellar Empire period

Against the powers of a sometime hostile Empire and always dangerous universe, the Order of Navigators historically applied the techniques of manipulation in depth. No plan instigated by the thinkers of Algol lacked alternate avenues to success.
—Nav (Bishop) Julianus Mullerium,
Anticlericalism in the Age of the Star Kings,
middle Second Stellar Empire period

The Technician appeared in the chapel of the starship as the remainder of the Five were completing their devotions. He was impatient and scarcely had the grace to wait until the position was sung. But when, at last, the cowled Navigators stood and made the sign of the Star in benediction, he stepped forward and said angrily, "I cannot make him respond. The Vulk's meddling has broken his conditioning."

The Preacher shrugged and bowed his head. "Then it is the will of God."

"Nothing of the sort," the Tactician said harshly. "What went wrong?"

"Even with the resonance of the locator in the girl, I still couldn't make him respond. But it isn't the *equipment's* fault. No one warned me a Vulk would be altering the parameters."

"This doesn't hold out much hope for *afterward*," the Logician murmured.

"What happens afterward is only of importance if we can make the change, brother," the Psychologist said. "We *must* bring them together."

"My thanks for stating the obvious," the Tactician said sarcastically.

"Peace," the Preacher said. "Peace, brothers. This will accomplish nothing."

The Psychologist drew back his cowl, baring a gray tonsured head and cold, brightly intelligent eyes. "I simply meant that if the boy refuses to go to Nyor, then Nyor must come to him."

"Can it be done?" the Logician asked.

The Psychologist looked at the Tactician. "It is relatively a military matter. *Can* it be done?"

"Yes, I think so. We can draw priests from sanctuaries in Jersey and Connecticut. There is a starship available."

"But the Imperial troops?"

The Tactician gave a harsh laugh. "It is always some saint's day. Anthony, Roosevelt, Crispian—someone. And what Vyks will interfere with a religious procession?"

"Very risky," the Technician said.

"Since your machines have failed us, I don't see, brother, that we have a choice," the Tactician said.

"And what about Aurora?" the Preacher asked. "I mean what about it *now*, or *tomorrow?* The Gonlani-Rhad are space-borne. Are we to let them attack Star Field and the Auroran sanctuary while we wait for Torquas?"

The Tactician addressed the Technician. "Can you get a message through to the sanctuary—and to Nyor?"

"The omens are good," the Technician replied unctuously.

"Spare me the religious mumbo jumbo, brother. Does your infernal machinery work that well? Can we count on it?"

The Preacher murmured a silent prayer for God to forgive the Tactician's worldliness.

"It *has* been working—as you put it—*that* well," the Technician said, offended.

The Psychologist, listening to the acrimony in his colleagues' voices, thought: *This is what comes of elitism. This is what one becomes when one has hyperspatial radio and nuclear power while the masses live in "safe" ignorance. The mighty become petty and spend their time in quarrels that accomplish nothing. We, the Princes of the Order,—what are we now? A quintet of dyspeptic old men, snapping at one another. Do we deserve for the plan to succeed? Should the Order have the power its success will give us?*

"We have been receiving reports from Nyor for the last three hours. Veg Tran embarked the Vegan division last night. He is coming on with the Vyks now. The first elements of the Vegans will reach Aurora in ten hours or less," the Technician said.

"Star Field or the sanctuary?" the Tactician asked.

"Our informant couldn't discover the first objective," the Technician said.

"It will be the sanctuary," the Logician said. "There's no other course for Tran to follow. He knows about the nuclear project there."

"Then the sanctuary must use the meson-screen," the Tactician said positively.

"It has never been tested," the Logician cautioned.

"It worked for the ancients. It will work for the Order."

The Logician raised his eyes to the vaulted overhead of the chapel. "Such faith is rewarding."

"Is there another option?" the soldierly Tactician demanded.

The others remained silent.

"It might mean the destruction of a starship," the Preacher said in a low voice.

"It almost certainly will," the Technician said.

"Sacrilege," said the Preacher. "May the Star forgive us!"

"The Order comes first," the Tactician said loudly, "Before all things."

"Before God?"

"Tran's soldiers can't be allowed to take the Auroran sanctuary."

"No." The Preacher surrendered sadly.

"Well, then?"

"But the loss of life? The troops on board? Our own Navigators?"

"Damn it!" the Tactician burst out. "What would you have us do, then?"

None of the Five had an answer.

Presently the Psychologist said. "If Kynan reaches the sanctuary first—? The screen takes hours to generate. What if it is *his* starship it destroys?"

The Tactician's face was rock-hard, like the face of an idol. "There is risk in every plan."

The Preacher made the sign of the Star on his breast. There were tears forming in his old eyes. "We are condemning our souls to everlasting fire," he murmured. "But if that is what our Order demands, then so be it."

The Tactician looked around him. "Are we agreed?"

The Technician and the Psychologist looked at one another. "Let it be so," the Psychologist said.

The Five turned, all taken by the same ingrained instinct, to look at the Star altar at the end of the chapel transept. The stellar image looked dull and metallic, inert, simply a piece of metal formed by men. There was no holy spirit here, the Preacher thought sadly.

The Tactician, the soldier, was very much in command now. "Are we all in agreement, then?" he asked again.

The Princes of the Order nodded slowly and murmured, "Amen."

"Very well," the Tactician said, turning to the Technician. "Send the messages. At once."

Chapter Fifteen

—hyperspatial radio transmissions from starships in intersystem transit may be dispatched only when the speed of the transmitting vessel is in the 10^{12} kps to 10^{32} kps range. Interrupter coils of the Mark XVII series now in use on board most Imperial naval vessels will draw only minimal power impulses from the propulsion cores, and thus the velocity of the transmission will be unaffected by the course or speed of the sending ship. Impulse velocity may be approximated by the formula P^{22} (Sv), where P = parsecs and SV = velocity of the sending vessel in kilometers per second. To all intents and purposes, then, hyperspatial radio transmissions may be considered instantaneous within a range of 10^{30} parsecs.
       —Golden Age fragment found at Station One,
        Astraris. Believed to be part of a First
        Empire Imperial naval field manual

The words of the gods streak the sky, burn the night.
They shriek below the stars, and above the wind
The god Galacton falls.
We hear his death wail
Not with our ears but with the fear in our hearts.
Dark gods of night, save us from sin.
       —Chant from the *Book of Warls*,
        Interregnal Period

* * *

High in the stratosphere of a dozen worlds on the helical path between the starship of the Five and the third planet of the star Sol, hyperspatial transmission ionized the widely separated molecules of air.

In the time of the First Empire, these sparkling, instantaneous displays were commonplace. But in this age, they were all but unknown.

On a planet of vast grain fields circling the star Bellatrix, a farmer raised his eyes to the fading light of day in the sky and saw, for an instant only, a streak of diamond light from horizon to horizon. He paused in his work of gathering sheaves and made the sign of the Star on his breast.

On the satellite of a methane giant orbiting Procyon, a fur trapper watching the sky from beside a low-burning fire saw the glittering beam, like a rent in the fabric of heaven. He remembered his father's father reading to the family from the *Book of Warls* and shivered as though the ghost of a warlock had set foot on his grave-to-be.

A warman on sentry duty on the battlements of a fortress in Tau Bootis saw the gem streak, and a fisherman alone on the Southern Sea of Achernar Three; a war party on the second planet of Deneb Kaitos, and a pair of lovers on the fourth planet of Alpha Draconis.

All across the galaxy, at one particular instant in time, the ionized upper air of a dozen worlds recorded the Five's message to Earth.

Alone but for his personal guard, Torquas XIII lay in drugged sleep in the Empire Tower in the city of Nyor.

His dreams were murky, confused. He slept uneasily, discontented with himself and his life.

Microseconds after the impulses left the hull of the inconceivably distant starship, they touched the rotating dish of an antenna in the Jersey sanctuary of the Order of Navigators. The hour on Earth, at that longitude, was minutes after the second hour of the morning.

As the watch cried the "All's well" for the third hour, a black barge bearing the spaceship and star blazon of the Theocracy touched the riverfront piers of Tel-Manhat. Fifteen cowled priests of the Order disembarked and moved, in slow, chanting procession, through the sleeping city. The few Nyori awakened by the processional peered fearfully through drawn shutters at the funereal parade.

At half past the hour, the Navigators had reached the citadel and were filing, three abreast, into the outer corridors and lower levels of the Empire Tower. The warmen on duty, Vyks and a few Rhad, being the most devout soldiers in the Empire—men who had been disturbed by the AbasNav ascendancy and the banishing of priests from the court—welcomed the solemn intruders and knelt, extending their weapons for the Navigators' blessings.

The Navigator Superior of the Jersey sanctuary carried his staff of office: an ebony rod topped by the metallic representation of the holy Star. The symbol went before the cowled and robed procession like a battle standard.

In the Galacton's antechamber, the Navigators were confronted by the captain of the Palace Guard, the Galacton's Chamberlain, and a squad of Vykan infantry.

"We will see the Galacton," the Navigator superior said.

The Chamberlain, an AbasNav party member, objected.

"At this time of the morning it is quite impossible, priest."

The courtier's manner was rude. He found himself astonished at the insolence of these prayer mumblers. His astonishment made him careless with his tongue. The Vyk soldiers shifted uneasily. On Vyka, the power of the Order was an article of faith. They resented the Chamberlain's manner.

"It must be so. We will see him now," the superior said, with that assurance peculiar to clerics.

"I've never heard of such damned cheek," the courtier sputtered. "Clear off, all of you, at once, or I shall have you thrown into the street."

"Priests have always had the right of access to the King-Emperor at any time, Chamberlain," the Vykan captain said uncomfortably. "Since Glamiss's time it has been so. It is their right."

"Captain," the Chamberlain said loftily. "I don't intend to continue this unseemly squabble in the Galacton's private rooms. You are relieved. Report to the guardroom at once and have Captain Veg Rollan come to me here."

The Vykan troopers made undisciplined noises, and the Chamberlain's temper rose. His face reddened, and he gave the order again.

The Navigator superior interceded. Reversing his staff, he began the chant of excommunication.

The Chamberlain, though an AbasNav, was a recently convinced unbeliever. His red face grew suddenly very pale.

The Vykan captain spoke. "Holy Father, it's my duty to guard the Galacton."

The superior stopped the chant and said, "We are priests, my son. We are here for the King-Emperor's good."

"I accept your word, holy Father." The captain caught the shaken Chamberlain by the arm and moved him aside. Chanting the hymn to the Star, the fifteen Navigators filed slowly into the dark sleeping chamber of the Galacton.

At the fourth hour, the Navigators reappeared. With them, now shorn and wearing a rough cassock, his feet bare, walked Torquas.

The priests were silent. The Galacton alone chanted the verses of the Act of Contrition.

His eyes were dark and inward-looking, his movements slow and deliberate. Before leaving the Tower he spoke only to the Chamberlain. His words, as reported by that badly frightened official, were: "I go to meet my father's Sun." From this, it was concluded that the King-Emperor, escorted by the Navigators of the Jersey sanctuary, was about to undertake a retreat on one of the Vykan planets, since Vyka was the only object in the galaxy that could be properly described as "his father's Sun." The Chamberlain, fearful to the bottom of his AbasNav heart and certain that had General Veg Tran not been off-world at this particular time the Galacton would never have gone with the priests, dispatched a message to Tran disclaiming any responsibility for the strange event. The message went by Imperial courier starship, giving the Chamberlain ample time to convert most of his holdings into cash and portables and depart for his estates in Fomalhaut. He hoped with all his being that General Veg Tran would be too busy for the next few months to come searching for him.

The Lady Florian, however, was more clever than the Chamberlain. She translated the Galacton's farewell differently, though even she, gossiping for hours about it with Sebastian, the Polari cyborg, could make no *true* sense of it. For what Torquas, under strong hypnotic suggestion from the superior of the Jersey sanctuary, had said, of course, was: "I go to meet my father's son."

Chapter Sixteen

I believe, dearest heart, that there will come a time when all men everywhere are free from fear and want; when all men will touch the face of God and share the old knowledge of the Ancients and the new knowledge that is sure to come. Then will the star kings and the priests and warlocks be blessedly forgotten. But we cannot wait for such a time, Queen, for it is far, far off. Ours is an age of faith and iron, and so it will be for our lifetime and for the lifetime of our children's children.
—From the letters of Kier of Rhada to Queen
Ariane, early Second Stellar Empire period

Students of the AbasNav movement have equated it with the legendary Know-Nothing Party of the American period of the Dawn Age. Others have suggested that the AbasNavs became disaffected in the time of the late Torquans, when it became generally known among the nobles of the Empire that the Navigators were rediscovering the dangerous knowledge of Golden Age science and reserving it for themselves. Clerical historians, of course, dispute this, and . . .
—Nav (Bishop) Julianus Mullerium,
Anticlericalism in the Age of the Star Kings,
middle Second Stellar Empire period

* * *

The strength of the AbasNav movement has been grossly exaggerated. The anticlericals of the Torquan Age were always few in number and vague in doctrine. Their so-called "power" derived exclusively from the ambition of one man, the ruthless and daring General Alain Veg Tran, who mercilessly used Imperial force to...

—Varus Milenis, *The New Renaissance*,
late Second Stellar Empire period

The starship's penetration of the atmosphere sent a rolling sonic boom over a million square kilometers of autumn forest and grassland, the virgin territories of Aurora's southern continent.

A Rim world, Aurora had few population centers. The three main cities had been built, time out of mind, on the seacoasts of the North Temperate Sea. A world of farms and herdsmen, the planet was ruled from Star Field and garrisoned by territorial troops, companies of native Aurorans who had served their time with the Imperial armies and retired to this peaceful planet of fields and woodlands on the boundaries of the Rhadan Palatinate.

Kynan's planetfall had been deliberately chosen, an ocean and continent away from the occupied lands and a thousand kilometers from the isolated complex of monasteries, chapels, and laboratories of the sanctuary.

In Janessa's grandfather's time, the Order had been ceded extraterritorial rights to several thousand square kilometers of land between the Janus River and the Great Inland Sea of the southern continent—the largest body of fresh water on the planet.

Kynan's holy books noted the planetary longitude and latitude, but since neither he nor any of his three juniors had ever visited the Aurora sanctuary, the exact location of the place was questionable. The holy books, containing thousands of planetary charts copied from the fragmentary records of the First Empire, were not always exact.

Kynan reclined now in the First Pilot's command station, observing directly through the polarized walls of the bridge.

The land three thousand meters below blazed with the colors of the Auroran fall: dark greens, red golds, brilliant yellows. In the crease of an unnamed mountain range, a river shone like molten silver in the afternoon light. The distant horizon blended with slightly greenish sky that was hazed, cloudless, empty. No sign of human habitation marred the vast stillness below.

Brother Evart, at the power console, was reaching the end of his power sequence litany: chanting the settings to the junior priests on the thrust controls.

"Energy Point Zero Three, Brother Pius."

Pius, being the youngest of the juniors and only sixteen years old, was excited by the nearness of the planetary surface. Starships did not normally travel this close to the ground unless fully manned by experienced Navigators. It had been found that the planetary effects tended to make control difficult, and starships had crashed to extinction in atmospheric flight. "Energy Point Zero Three, for the glory of the Star," Pius intoned.

"Let's get down to one hundred meters off the contours, Evart," Kynan ordered.

Evart's expression betrayed his opinion of the order. Contour flying with a starship of a million metric tons took confidence only a fully consecrated First Pilot such as Kynan possessed.

Kynan was young enough to explain his command—a thing an older priest would never have done. "I want to approach the sanctuary at low altitude, Brother Evart. There are apt to be vessels from Gonlan over the enclave. I want to come in low and after dark."

"Yes, First Pilot. But won't navigation be difficult?"

Kynan gave Evart what he hoped was a cold and commanding look.

"Mea culpa, First Pilot," the junior said humbly. "Energy Level to Point Zero Zero One, Brother Pius."

"Zero Zero One, Blessed be the Name," the youngster replied, adjusting the banked rheostats.

The land below seemed to come closer, become more detailed. Kynan could see the white-barked trees and the gray faces of molded granite cliffs. A late afternoon breeze sent ripples across the reddish mountain meadows. The silvery river showed the riffles and shallows of an Alpine course. In the distance, the water plunged over a granite face to form a waterfall of feathery beauty.

The starship descended to the one-hundred-meter level, and Kynan gave the order for hovering flight. It was late afternoon, planetary time. Aurora's period of rotation gave a day, at this time of year, of twenty-nine Earth Standard Hours. The Auroran sun slanted across the peaceful wilderness below, casting long shadows into the ravines between the massive hills and mountains. Kynan could see brightly plumed birds soaring on long, tapering wings. These hawks, with wing spans of ten meters or more, were the largest form of life indigenous to Aurora. Until the coming of the First Empire colonists, the great birds had dominated the planet. In fact, Kynan realized with a touch of uncharacteristic humility, they *still* owned most of Auroran air. The total human population of Aurora was well under eleven million. It was but one of the many facts one considered when it was said that man had "conquered" the known galaxy.

Kynan went to the plotting boards and began to lay out a course for the Great Inland Sea. It lay more than seven hours away at subsonic speed. Kynan had no intention of racing across even these uninhabited lands preceded by a sonic boom to warn all possible watchers of his coming.

He had almost completed his task when the clangor of an alarm shattered the busy quiet of the bridge.

In ancient times an alarm had been thought to be a ghostly manifestation of the greetings exchanged by two starships. Certain Navigators had contended that the ships were not only sacred objects, but actually living beings, and that they spoke to one another through the medium of the alarm. But Navigator Anselm Styr (before his researches carried him into the pit of heresy) had proved that the starships, miraculous though they might be, were but artifacts of the Golden Age and the alarm but a device intended to prevent collisions at sublight speeds.

An actual alarm, however, was a rare and unsettling occasion, for hidden bells took up a clangor, the ship's identifiers went into clattering action, and information sequences began to appear on read-outs above the First Pilot's console. In addition to this, a three-dimensional representation of the danger area with all it contained materialized as a holograph in the space usually occupied by the stellar navigational globes.

The result of the present alarm was a startled reaction of prayer from Evart and Brothers Pius and Clement, together with an indistinct image of five starships in the holograph. The lack of clarity, Kynan knew, was caused by atmospheric interference—normally, starships did not exchange Warnings except in space.

The lighted identification signals marched across the read-out screen: registration numbers, nationality, tonnage, speed, and direction for each of the intercepted vessels. All were Imperial starships, and all were in the process of reentry for a planetfall the ship's computer placed near the Great Inland Sea.

Instinctively, Kynan raised his eyes to stare at the emptiness of the sky above the transparent curve of the polarized hull. There was nothing to be seen, of course, for the new arrivals were a hundred kilometers and more above. And even as he stood, the sound of the warning bells died, the holograph faded and the computer fell silent as the Imperial vessels raced on around the vast curve of Aurora.

"Imperials, First Pilot!" Evart exclaimed unnecessarily.

Brother Clement, a more silent and perhaps more thoughtful young man than Evart, put Kynan's thought into words: "Did *they* detect *us*, First Pilot?"

"Perhaps not. We are very low, and the ground returns might blank out our transmissions." It was a possibility only. He could not be certain that their presence on Aurora now remained a secret.

Kynan gave Evart the course for the sanctuary. "Stay subsonic and one hundred meters above the terrain. When we reach the Janus River, send Clement to fetch me."

"As you say, First Pilot. It will be done."

Kynan rubbed a hand across his eyes. His head still pained him, and though the illogical urge to lift ship and run for Earth was less, it was still present: an unexplained and frightening demand, like an alien presence in his mind. He wished fervently that the wise Gret were with him. A Vulk, with his strange knowledge of men's minds, might be able to sort this out properly. But Gret was parsecs away, at Melissande, or perhaps on Rhada. There was nothing to be done but to go on, hoping to forestall what seemed sure to come.

But *Imperials!* How did they know what was happening on Aurora? And what did they intend?

"Are you still unwell, First Pilot?" Evart asked worriedly.

"Do not trouble yourself, Evart," Kynan said, feeling the weight of responsibility for far more than he could have ever foreseen on that day he started for Melissande.

He made the sign of the Star and left the bridge, seeking Baltus the warlock.

He found the warlock in his quarters. "Five Imperial starships passed over us a short time ago. They are on a course for the sanctuary," he said without preamble.

Baltus pulled his beard and looked thoughtful. "There is something very wrong, I think."

Kynan shrugged. "We knew we could expect some reaction from the Empire as soon as the Gonlani-Rhad threatened to attack Aurora."

Baltus raised his eyebrows. "Naturally. But the time element is all wrong, isn't it? Crespus and LaRoss must still be gathering the warband at home. Or at best, only now loading the starships. How did the Imperials know trouble was brewing here?"

Kynan gnawed his lip and considered. Suspicion was growing.

"Only if someone who was at Star Field when the festival was attacked told them," Baltus said. "It is the only way."

"Or if Imperials were themselves involved. Isn't that what you are thinking?"

The warlock shook his head. "Not exactly, Nav Kynan. I've studied the Torquans root and branch. Torquas X might have staged such an incident. Torquas the Poet, never. But there is someone who could have done it, and who would—given the proper intelligence and opportunity."

"The AbasNavs?"

The warlock nodded. "General Veg Tran. We get precious little news of the Empire out here on the Rim, but it is general knowledge that the AbasNav party has been losing adherents in recent years. The people of the Inner Marches think Tran too extreme—for all that he's a military hero and popular with the aristocracy. But any sort of Imperial campaign on Aurora would give the perfect opportunity to pick a serious quarrel with the Order. All he would have needed to know was when the princes of the Gonlani-Rhad would be at Star Field. A commando force could do the rest and provide the perfect *causus belli*. It is traditional for the Navigators of each nation to help defend it in time of war. What better chance to bring about an open break between the Order and the Empire?"

Kynan leaned against the bulkhead and tried to clear his aching head. "Two things bother me, Baltus. First—wouldn't even General Veg Tran be taking a tremendous risk *personally* in trying to create a situation between the Empire and the Order? I don't think the people of the Empire would support an anticlerical war. There's no reason for it."

The warlock said sadly, "You would say that because you are a Navigator, Kynan. There are a great many who think that the Order is keeping the old knowledge for itself—for its own aggrandizement."

"That's not true!" Kynan declared hotly.

"In a sense, it *is* true. It isn't black magic, no matter what the ignorant believe. It is a body of scientific truth that could be vastly expanded if it were not for the dead hand of the clergy—"

"No more, Baltus. On peril of your soul, *no more.*" The young priest's face was flushed with anger.

"Forgive me, Kynan. I go too far," the warlock said quietly.

Kynan felt a flood of contrition. This man was his bond-father's friend. He was no follower of Antistar, nor even a priest-baiter. He was simply a questing intelligence hungry for knowledge. And, in truth, much knowledge was withheld by the Order on the theory that unrestrained access to the marvels of science had brought civilization to the Dark Time.

Kynan laid a hand on the warlock's shoulder. "I have no right to be angry with you, Baltus. And there is truth in what you say. But the Order is holy. I am not the one to question what I have spent my lifetime learning. Of this you may be sure—the Order of Navigators means well—it wishes no man harm."

"I believe that, Kynan. And I should have been more respectful, I know. But for the Order's custody of the old ways, we would have gone from savagery to savagery and the Dark Time would never have ended. But I only point out that there *is* discontent with the Order, and not all of it from people who are willing to name themselves AbasNavs. If General Tran can provoke the Order—and if he can resist it *physically*—the old technique of interdiction and excommunication may not be enough to stop something that could spread, a bloody religious war— I shouldn't like to think about that."

The warlock was right, painfully, deadly right, Kynan admitted to himself. For a moment his spirit rebelled. Why *me?* Of all the Navigators in the Empire, why was Kynan of Gonlan here, now, in this time and place?

He remembered the spinning, beautiful, frightening visions of only hours ago: the world of men between his hands, the swirling star clouds like a dust of diamonds against the black emptiness of infinity, *infinity—*

He covered his face with his hands and thought again: *Why me? I'm only a simple priest, and a very young one at that—Then why?*

The warlock's voice was concerned. "Are you all right? Has it come again?"

Kynan shook his head and said, "No. I am well." He began to pace the softly humming deck of the compartment. "There was something else," he said.

"About General Veg Tran?"

"About Imperials on Aurora. Now."

The warlock waited, not wanting to put his own thoughts into words, for he was a loyal citizen of Gonlan.

"Someone. Some one of *us,*" Kynan began heavily, "informed the Imperial general of what happened at Star Field. No, that's not right. I think it was by General Veg Tran's order that the attack on Star Field was made. And that means that someone, one of the Gonlani-Rhad, plotted it with him." He paused, and it was painful for him to continue, because one part of the puzzle had begun to unravel and the unwinding skein was baring something ugly. "It wasn't Crespus. He wasn't at Star Field—and he's too straightforward an old soldier to become involved in something so—so dishonorable."

"Not Tirzah, either," Baltus offered. "Tirzah is a feudal old savage who thinks he is living in the time of Kier, but he loved your bond-father like a brother."

"LaRoss, then," Kynan said, the words like stones in his mouth. "Or my bond-brother."

"You have been away from Melissande a long time, Kynan," Baltus said. "When you say LaRoss, you say Karston. When you say Karston, you say LaRoss. The heir and the First Minister have grown very close since Kreon began to grow old and difficult."

"Could my brother *actually* countenance parricide, Baltus? Could *he?*" Kynan asked bleakly.

"It is not an uncommon thing in royal families, Nav Kynan. Sons grow impatient with aging kings."

"But my own bond-brother—can I believe that of him?"

The warlock said, "The poison fed Kreon may not have been intended to do more than incapacitate him while Karston or LaRoss took out the warband." Baltus did not for one moment believe this, but he could see how the thought of his brother actually involved in treason, regicide, and conspiracy was affecting the young Navigator. Kynan looked physically ill.

Kynan was too honest to accept the palliative the warlock was offering. "No," he said. "If it is as we think, then Karston is guilty." The dark blue eyes turned almost metallic, and the tone of voice was bitter and royal. "And if he is guilty, warlock—if my bond-brother is guilty of our star king's death—I promise by the Star and by all that I hold dear and holy, I will kill him with my own hands."

The warlock made the sign of the Star, certain that he had heard a death sentence pronounced on Karston the Proud, prince of the Gonlani-Rhad. "Let it be so," he said softly.

The Warning triggered by the passing of the Imperial squadron through the stratosphere of Aurora was detected elsewhere that evening.

On the shores of the Inland Sea, where the forests grew down almost to the water's edge, the starship of the Five lay aground at the Janus River delta. The great vessel, handled with consummate skill, had been floated into a hiding place beneath the huge trees. It rested now, inert, radiating no signals, as the last light of Aurora's sun sank into the still waters of the great, desolate lake.

The starship had been grounded athwart the only land approach to the Navigator's enclave, which lay but half a dozen kilometers to the north, along the shore. As the sky darkened with the onset of night, the cowled Tactician, standing in the open valve of the starship, could see the faint luminosity of the meson screen shimmering beyond the crest of a low-lying hill. The sight gave him a deep, almost savage, satisfaction. The sanctuary, with its complex of uranium-enrichment plants, laboratories, ore-reduction facilities, chapels, and dormitories, was now invulnerable. The forces of the Empire could attack it only at their peril.

From within the starship came the sounds of the Technician's tracking equipment. Both Kynan's vessel and the starship approaching from deep space were on the plotting tables, their tracks converging: Kynan's slowly, across the map of Aurora's southern continent—the ship of the Jersey Navigators plunging planetward at a speed only now below that of light. The starship carrying the befuddled Torquas would arrive first, within the hour. The Tactician tensed with nervous anticipation. The plan was approaching its critical point. Within a day's time, perhaps less, the power of the Order over all the vastness of the Empire would be complete. There would be an end to constant disorder, an end to the petty quarrels of star kings and nobles, an end—praise be to the holy Star—to the bloodshed and suffering of centuries.

The Tactician breathed deeply of the evening air of Aurora. Such was the bounty of God and his holy Star that there were in the galaxy literally millions of planets like this one: rich, silent, waiting for the cultivating hand of man and his works. To this end did all Navigators work and worship, when all was said and done: to bring man peacefully into his kingdom; to spread a disciplined and devout humankind throughout a galaxy of unbelievable richness and beauty.

The Order Militant would see to it, the Tactician thought, making the sign of the Star unconsciously on his breast.

"You surprise me, brother," the Preacher said at his shoulder.

The Tactician turned. "Why?"

"I wouldn't have expected to see you praying."

The Tactician studied the older man's face. "I am a soldier and a prince of the Order. But I am also a priest. Why should it surprise you that I act as one?"

The Preacher stood beside his colleague, looking through the great trees to the darkening sky above the Inland Sea. "It is very beautiful, isn't it." He seemed to expect no reply and received none. Presently, he said, "The Imperial squadron will land on their next orbit."

The Tactician's face was steely under the dark cowl. "Let them."

"Shouldn't they have some warning? Are we to let men die in the meson screen?"

"It is hard, but there must be a lesson."

"And the Navigators on board those ships?"

The Tactician's voice was as hard as his expression. "We all dedicate ourselves when we join the Order. We pledge our lives."

"It is your specialty that makes you so unbending, brother," the Preacher said sadly. "May the Star forgive you."

"It is for the Order," the Tactician said stonily.

The Preacher looked at the soft radiance in the air: it outlined the forested ridge like some strange witch fire. It brought a shiver of superstitious dread. Once every starship had been capable of generating that destructive power. But the machines that created it had been useless for two thousand years. Yet now, the seekers in the Aurora sanctuary had produced it again—with great cumbersome machines no starship could carry, it was true—but produced it, nonetheless. And soon, men would rediscover still another of the deadly wonders of the First Empire's dreadful genius. The meson screen absorbed the energy that maintained a starship in flight, converted the magnificent, holy vessel into simply a million metric tons of metal and human flesh and blood. A starship caught in a meson pattern simply ceased to be a starship. It would fall like a stone. Such a thing was horrifying—to the Preacher, blasphemous, the work of Antistar.

"Is there no other way, brother?" the Preacher asked. "Couldn't Kynan command the Veg?"

"Kynan isn't here yet, nor is Torquas. In any case, the Veg would probably not obey unless something terrifying happens first. The meson screen will provide the instructive lesson."

The Preacher ran an almost loving hand over the ancient metal of the starship's valve. "To kill a starship can only be a heinous sin, brother. It was never part of the plan."

"Any plan must be flexible. And those who implement it must be ruthless. Think of the purpose," the soldier-priest said harshly.

"The end justifies the means?"

"If you like."

The Preacher breathed deeply of the forest smells. In the distance, a great hawk uttered a mournful hunting cry. The tops of the trees, twenty meters overhead, sighed with a breath of the evening wind from the Inland Sea. "May God forgive us," the old man muttered.

Before the Tactician could make a bitter reply, the voice of the Technician called from inside. "Starship entering the atmosphere. One track. It is the ship from Earth."

The Tactician turned away from his contemplation of the deepening dusk and said to the Preacher, "Come, brother. We had best make ready to receive the last king of the Universe."

Chapter Seventeen

*This wimpled, whining, purblind, wayward boy,/ . . .
Regent of love rhymes, lord of folded arms,/The
anointed sovereign of sighs and groans,/ Liege of all
loiterers and malcontents.*
—Attributed to one William Shakespeare,
poet of the pre-Golden Age period.
Fragment found at Tel-Avon, Earth

*What we know of history tells us that hereditary
kingship is not the best of all possible methods of governing the nations of men. Yet what are we to do? We
can but follow the kings, obey our consciences, and
trust in God.*
—Emeric of Rhada, Grand Master of Navigators,
early Second Stellar Empire period

For the first time in a life filled with uncertainties, Torquas of Vyka feared not for his life, but for his immortal soul.

The Navigators who had almost literally abducted him from Nyor had given him no peace on this journey. They had come upon him in the Empire Tower while he lay in a half stupor of drugs, and for a time he had been hard put to know whether he was living a dream or reality had become hallucination.

Hemp and the drugs prepared by his warlock often brought fantasies of great beauty and satisfaction, dreams in which he was, indeed, the great captive genius he wanted so to be—a poet whose lines made the very skies blaze with transcendental brilliance. But sometimes the dreams were less gratifying, and there were great insects on the walls, and flaming cauldrons where he saw the faces of his people cursing him, and other nightmares too horrible to contemplate.

And it seemed to him that the Navigators had come to him in one such hallucination and had spoken to him of duty and redemption, and—he had the impression—of retribution, too. They had taken him from his bed and shaved his beard and cropped his hair, washing the stain from his lips and the kohl from his eyes. Then they had dressed him in homespun, like any pilgrim, and had taken him—

Where? He found it difficult to remember. The river. He remembered crossing the dark waters of the West River. There had been a starship waiting, and he had slept suddenly, a dreamless, weary sleep that was somehow a relief to his fearful, anxious heart.

That was the tragedy of being Galacton, he thought with infinite self-pity. One was consumed by fear and dare not show it. Fear of everything: plotters, assassins. Fear of friends and enemies. Fear of ambitious relatives, and of wars and revolutions and *responsibilities*—

But presently he had found that the hallucination persisted. Or it was no hallucination. He was, in fact, a passenger on a Navigators' starship, bound for some unknown destination, surrounded by sallow-faced, unlovely priests in black clericals; all of them chanting and praying and treating him with an unroyal mixture of deference, contempt, pity, and disapproval.

It was unbelievable. He was *Galacton*. Who would dare to take him where he had no wish to go? Who dared preach to him of duty and kingship? Who kept him from his blessed drugs and colored lights and wild music? Who but the Navigators, the black, funereal, sober, terrible *Navigators?*

Was Tran right, after all? Wasn't this part of a black plague of priests overrunning the Empire, armed with dreadful magical powers?

And yet, when the surging waves of panic receded, he felt a strange peace. No one could reach him now. Florian couldn't bedevil him with her razor tongue. The warmen couldn't press him to display himself to the soldiers and even risk himself in war. No one even *knew* where he was. In space. Somewhere, far beyond the last stars visible from Earth. Only the Navigators could have taken the King of the Universe from his golden haven and brought him out here, among the stars that he owned, that the kings of Vyka had won for him and for all the Vykans—forever.

But was it forever? The starship was landing. He could feel the life in the ancient, magical ship subsiding, dying. The Navigators had not merely brought him out among the stars to recapture his health and his soul. They had brought him to some *place,* for some *reason*.

He could hear the footsteps of still more black priests approaching down the long companionway toward his chambers.

His fear began again.

The land below lay indistinct in the starlight. Occasionally, Kynan could make out the faint reflection of the Janus. The river was broadening as the starship moved slowly nearer to the Inland Sea.

"That luminosity on the horizon, First Pilot," Brother Pius asked tentatively. "Have you ever seen anything like it before?"

"Is it sky-glow from the sanctuary?" Evart asked.

It resembled no city sky-glow Kynan had ever seen. The night was still and clear. The sky was a Rim sky, with few stars and a well-defined ribbon of milky brightness defining the edge of the great galactic lens. But there were no clouds to catch the reflected light of a city. Instead, the air itself seemed to pulse with faint illumination, like an Aurora Borealis.

In a way, it reminded the Navigator of the pulsing ionization of the air that surrounded a starship in flight. Yet this was far too extensive and dim for it to be that familiar phenomenon. That its source was the enclave, however, he did not doubt. Across the next low range of hills lay the Great Inland Sea.

It had been Kynan's intention to fly the starship to the edge of the sea and approach the sanctuary in slow atmospheric flight. Now he was not so certain. There was something indefinably menacing about that dark, throbbing radiation.

He leaned forward, inclining his pilot's couch so that he could study the dark terrain below. The tops of the great trees shone blackish green in the light cast by the ionization of the air surrounding the starship's hull. "Slow us down, Brother Evart," he orderd. "Two percent thrust."

"Thrust Two, for the glory of God," Evart intoned, making the adjustments.

The starship hung almost motionless above the treetops, tons of superhard steel and dural floating, drifting on the inshore wind.

"First Pilot!" Brother Clement exclaimed. "Look there! A light!"

Ahead and below, shining through the dark leaves of the forest tops, a single brilliant point of brightness gleamed. A signal laser. At the same moment Kynan's head began to ache again. It was as though something, or someone, were attempting to tamper with the very stuff of his brain. The impulse was indistinct, unformed, but the import of it was unmistakable: *Land at once.*

He scrubbed at his eyes and studied the pulsations of the signal beam. The message was in open code: "In the name of the Theocracy, you are to touch down immediately." Then followed the cascade of signals that identified him, Kynan, by name and rank. Only high members of the Order had access to such symbols or to the complex devices for creating a beam to send them.

Kynan was too disciplined a Navigator to question that imperative, commanding laser signal. For some reason beyond his understanding, there were Navigators down there in the dark forest, two hours' march from the Auroran sanctuary: Navigators old enough, exalted enough to give him orders. It was a thing he had been wishing for most devoutly—almost, he thought, making the sign of the Star on his black-clothed breast, a proper miracle.

"Stand by to touch down," he ordered.

"Here, First Pilot?" Evart asked fearfully.

Kynan favored him with an angry look. "Beyond the signal light," he said sternly.

"Mea culpa, First Pilot." Evart began to give orders for the landing sequence to Clement and Pius.

Kynan watched the treetops tensely, seeking a clearing. There was none. The starship drifted slowly over the winking, demanding laser beam. In the glow of ionization now, Kynan could make out the great humping backs of two starships aground, side by side. He could see the bare flesh of the huge trees the starships had broken like matchsticks as they touched down in this hidden place.

"Put her down through the trees, Brother Evart," he said.

"Amen, First Pilot," Evart murmured.

The humming of the ship's engines faded to an almost inaudible whisper. The keel touched the tops of the trees, and ionized particles seemed to set the leaves and branches alight with a cold fire that ran down the massive trunks to splash like molten gems on the soft soil of the forest floor.

The great starship settled, brushing the massive trees aside as though they were nothing, breaking the meters-thick trunks and pulping the uprooted stumps with tons of growing weight. Oddly shaped leaves brushed along the polarized curvature of the bridge, their skeletal structures shimmering with light.

"Touch down, First Pilot," Brother Pius reported.

Kynan could see the dark vaults of the forest stretching all around; he could feel the huge mass of the starship settling comfortably into the loamy ground, cradling itself into the soil.

"Stand-by sequence," he ordered.

"Preflight Energy Level, in the name of the Name," Evart ordered in his holier-than-thou tone.

"Holding pulse power," Pius replied shortly, his attention caught by the vastness of the mysterious forest into which they had penetrated.

Kynan eased himself from the pilot's couch. His head was throbbing again. Was it really the Vulk contact that had done this to him? Triad had never been a painful experience to him, but perhaps Gret had penetrated too deeply. The human mind was such a tangle of unknown skeins—

"Open the starboard valve in five minutes, Evart," he ordered.

"Are you going out alone, First Pilot?"

"I want you and the others to remain here. Hold preflight power and be ready to take the ship away if I do not return by morning." The protection of the starship was the first and most holy duty of any Navigator.

The three juniors inclined their heads and murmured an Ave Stella for his safety.

Kynan left the bridge and hurried to his quarters for his robe, cowl, and weapons. The ache behind his eyes was filling him with urgency.

Armed and cowled, his mail heavy on his breast, he sought Janessa. The girl was with the warlock in the corridor leading to the stables. She looked frightened, and Kynan felt a pang of remorse. He had been neglecting his ward. He had been too busy to keep her informed, and it was forbidden, of course, for an unconsecrated person to enter the control room of a starship. She burst into questions as he appeared.

"Where are we, Kynan? What is this place? Are we near Star Field? What's happened?"

Kynan silenced her with a hand on her shoulder. He spoke with some difficulty because his head was hurting badly. "We are in a forest near the Great Inland Sea. We saw a signal. There are two starships of the Order landed here. I am going to report to my superiors."

"But Star Field? The Gonlani strike force?" Her eyes were alight with patriotic concern for her city and her people.

"The strike force must be far behind us. But we *did* see a squadron of Imperials. I don't know yet what that means, but perhaps I can find out now."

Baltus said, "You say there are two starships of the Order here? What of the sanctuary?"

Kynan decided to say nothing about the mysterious light he had seen surrounding the Navigators' enclave. It wasn't wise to discuss everything freely with seculars, particularly warlocks.

"I must go immediately," he said. "Baltus, you must stay here with Janessa."

"We can't go with you?" the girl asked.

"Better not," Kynan said, moving away.

"You don't look well, Kynan," Baltus said.

"I will take Skua. It isn't far."

Kynan saw, with a sense of some pleasure, a look of deep concern on Janessa's face. He could not resist an impulse to touch her silvery blond hair. She came to him, pressed herself against his mailed chest, and kissed him. Baltus looked away with un-warlockish politeness.

Then Kynan stepped over the scuttle into the stable and called to Skua as the great valve began to dilate and the night smells of Aurora's forests seeped into the cavernous belly of the starship. For Janessa, the scent of the inland water, the great trees, and the wind were the odors of home. She watched the young Navigator saddle Skua and swing lightly to her back, and she was still standing at the bulkhead as horse and rider moved down the ramp and into the forest.

"You love him, princess?" Baltus asked quietly.

"He is my choice," she said simply.

The old war mare, moving lightly as a filly, picked her way with dainty steps through the rubble of fallen leaves and branches brought down by the starship's descent.

Kynan, his head still throbbing with sick pain, sat loosely in the saddle. The weight of his pistol and the sword slung across his back seemed to drag at him. His eyes hurt with the pressure of the steel cap and cowl on his forehead. Ahead, more than a kilometer from where his vessel had finally touched down, he could see the imperative pencil of light from the laser signal.

"To the light, Skua," he said.

"Yes, Ky-nan," the animal replied, bobbing her head and shaking her mane. She was rested but hungry: there had been no game for her since leaving Melissande. She hoped for battle and the rewards of a fight—the flesh of her alien cousins. But her primitive telepathy told her that there were no chargers ahead—only many men.

Kynan rode slackly. It seemed to him that the closer he came to the narrow beam of light in the forest, the more painful the ache in his skull became. He was seriously worried now, for it seemed to him that he had contracted, in some mysterious way, a terrible and possibly deadly ailment. There was madness in it, too. He was thinking of his visions, and of the crashing, demanding commands that seemed to burst unbidden into his consciousness. The whole business filled him with sadness: he had been raised a Rhad, after all, and the Rhad were among the most melancholy people in the galaxy. Their guest songs were filled with sad tales of broken love affairs and battles won only at the cost of hero's lives. Their sagas were laments and their melodies all in minor keys. It was said that the Rhad lived at the edge of the sky and grew sad because there were no more worlds left to conquer.

He moved through what appeared to be an immense, groined hall in which the giant trees were the columns, the tops, far overhead, the vaulted arches. It made him think of the great churches on Algol, the flaming Star symbol on the high altar, the echoing chants of the hidden choirs singing the Psalms and the ephemerides. He was filled with a great, weary love for the Order, which brought reason and religion into a universe teeming with angry men and nations.

He urged Skua to go a bit more quickly. He had been too long away from the comfort of his Order. What a relief it would be now to lay his burden down before superiors, to tell them what was happening and let them decide what should be done.

The mare's padded paws made no sound on the forest floor as she carried Kynan into the small clearing. The immense curving flank of a starship loomed overhead. Kynan raised his eyes to the open valve. There, with the light behind him, stood a prince of the Order. The Navigator could not make out the golden spaceship and star on the priest's breast, but no insignia was needed to mark this man as a high priest. There was fur edging on his cowl, and it seemed that he stood in a halo of brilliance from within the starship.

He looked down at the rider and spoke. "Come with me, Nav Kynan." His voice was sonorous, that of a man accustomed, for many years, to commanding.

Kynan dismounted, knelt on the ground, and made the sign

of the Star. "Bless me, Father," he said.

The older priest made the ritual sign and said, "Come quickly now, my son."

It did not occur to Kynan to wonder how the prince knew his name, or that he would be in these skies at this particular time. The ghostly knowledge of the Five was legendary. And this was, indeed, one of the fabled quintet of advisers to the Grand Master. The singular cut of his robes Kynan could now see made that plain. He was filled with awe and wonder but not surprise. It was right and reasonable that wherever in the galaxy trouble brewed, there would be the power of the Five to protect both the Order and the faithful.

Kynan said to Skua, "Wait for me."

The mare's blue-green eyes glittered in the light from the open valve. "Yes, Ky-nan. May I hunt? I hunger."

"Hunt, but don't go far."

The mare bared her teeth and wheeled to gallop into the forest.

The Tactician followed the colloquy between horse and man with interest. "A Rhadan horse. They are rare, Nav Kynan."

"Not in this part of the galaxy, Father. The Rhad sell them throughout all this province of the Empire."

It seemed to Kynan that the senior priest reacted coldly to his mention of the Empire, but he could have imagined it. His sickness was heavily upon him. He made his way up the ramp and presented himself to the great Navigator. "Blessings on the Five," he said respectfully.

The older man's eyebrows arched. His dark eyes glittered with intelligence and purpose. Never, thought Kynan devoutly, had he seen so commanding a face. Not even Kreon of Gonlan looked like this.

"So you know who I am," the Tactician said. "Very well, that is good. It will save much time. I am not the only one here, my son. *All* the Five are here. What we must do here tonight and when morning comes is that important to our Order. Do you understand me?"

"I hear you, Father," Kynan said humbly.

"We have names, my son. But we seldom use them. I am called simply the Tactician."

Kynan inclined his head, impressed. Tactician was the title

given the nearest thing to a supreme military commander extant in the Order of Navigators.

"Are you unwell, Kynan?"

"A fever of some sort, I think, Father. I seem to have contracted it on Gonlan."

The shrewd eyes narrowed. "Or from a Vulk, my son?"

By the holy Star, Kynan thought. *He even knows that!* Was there no limit to the power to know among the princes of the Order?

The Tactician took Kynan's arm and led him into the starship. As he walked, he spoke. "You were brought here for a purpose, Kynan. For a mighty purpose of immense importance to our Order. What you must do will require great sacrifice and courage. But always remember that you are of the Order. The Order is your strength, your courage, your purpose. It is your very reason for being. That is the way of the Navigator."

The words were both frightening and soothing to Kynan. He could feel the sheltering arms of the brotherhood of the Order enfolding him, sustaining him.

"History is a mighty stream, my son. It flows through time in mysterious ways known only to God and his holy Star. But there are choices to be made, changes that even mere men can sometimes, in God's great mercy, affect in history's flow. Do you understand that, Kynan?" He maintained his grip on Kynan's arm and went on, not waiting for an answer to his rhetorical question. "Occasionally, once in generations, there is a confluence of forces, a time of decision. In those times there is a nexus in which all change—all possibility of *different* history—is concentrated in one event—in one *individual.*"

He stopped before the star-blazoned door to the starship's bridge. Kynan had never seen such a door as this in a starship. It was something unknown in the construction of all the vessels in which he had served. The implication was enormous, staggering. This was a *new* thing, something *added* to the ancient, immortal vessels. To his young mind it was blasphemy, yet if it was countenanced here on the starship of the Five, it could not be unholy. The presence of the door and the symbol meant that the Order itself had rebuilt and modified a starship. It was incredible but true.

But what the Tactician said next was an even greater shock to Kynan.

"Twenty years ago such an event occurred, such a nexus was created. *You are such a nexus of power, Nav Kynan.*" Before Kynan could react to that astonishing statement, the Tactician had swung open the door to the control room, and Kynan faced the four remaining members of the Five.

The priest who seemed the oldest of the group rose and came forward. "I am the Theologian, Nav Kynan." The ghost of a smile touched the withered lips. "My colleagues sometimes call me the Preacher."

Kynan could only nod his head. He was unable to contain or control his spinning thoughts.

"Are you devout, my son? Are you a true son of the Order?"

"I believe so, Father," Kynan replied. His throat felt dry, and his voice sounded hoarse and unsteady.

"That is good. Because what you must do will demand all your devotion, all your ability to withstand temptation."

The Tactician said, "That is the Psychologist. That is the Logician. They are often at odds, just as the Preacher and I are. It is understood that this is so, for what we plan for the Order is never simple, and all voices must be heard before the Grand Master acts. And *that* is the Technician. Perhaps he can ease your pain."

Kynan now looked about in wonder to see that *many* new things had been incorporated into this starship. The bridge was filled with unfamiliar equipment, banks of it. "I don't understand you, Father," he said.

"I told you that you were a nexus, Kynan. This means that, since birth, you have been watched and cared for by the Order. Long before you finished your cadetship on Gonlan, you were a ward of the Navigators. It was the Order who brought you to Kreon—a true son of the faith. It was the Order who educated and trained you. You have been watched every day of your twenty years, Kynan—watched and guided and protected."

Kynan regarded the Tactician with an expression of complete confusion. The older man smiled and nodded. "It is so, my son. Believe it." The smile faded. "Days ago the Royal

Vulk of Rhada came near to discovering how this was done—and more dangerously, *why*. Since that time you have been suffering great pain, is that not so?"

"Yes, Father," Kynan said wonderingly.

"He came near to breaking your conditioning. He probed deeply in a kind of Triad—but with a much stronger mindtouch. What remained were the physical implants."

"The what?" Uncomprehending, Kynan frowned.

The Tactician said, "Show him."

The man known as the Technician walked to a machine and made an adjustment. Instantly, the throbbing ache in Kynan's skull ceased. For a moment he found it impossible to grasp the immense implications of what had happened in that moment.

He pushed off his cowl and steel cap. The casque clattered, rolling on the deck. Kynan pressed his fingertips to his head; he was trembling.

"*Surgical implants?*" he said raspingly.

"Since five days after your birth," the Technician said calmly. "They were made on the starship carrying you to Gonlan from Earth."

"As the plan progressed," the Tactician went on inexorably, "we found that we would need an amplifier near you. The choice was Janessa. She underwent an appendectomy at Star Field a year ago. She, too, was implanted."

The room seemed to rock around Kynan. He imagined tendrils of invisible wire lacing through his brain, through the soft pulpy gray of it, like metal veins and arteries—*controlling* him—like a *cyborg*—and they did something almost as bad to Janessa, to *Janessa*— "My God," he breathed. "Oh, my *God!*"

This, then, was the source of the wild dreams, the spinning galaxies, the crown of Earth—all of it . . .

His stomach churned with sickness. He clutched his violated skull with clawed fingers as though to tear the implants out with his nails.

"We would not have taken such liberties with a fellow human being, my son," the Tactician went on relentlessly, "but for your vital importance to the Empire and the Order. Your life has been our guarantee of survival—of *triumph*—in a hostile universe. And now we must enforce that guarantee. If you are a puppet—remember you are a puppet of the *Order*, of God, of the holy Star. Cling fast to your faith, my son—"

"My faith—" Kynan said in a voice like death. "My faith—"

"It has come to pass, my son, that the plan created so long ago—on the occasion of your birth, to be exact—*must* now go forward. And now, you shall see *how* and *why*." The Tactician strode to the blazoned door. The Preacher threw up his hands in protest. "By the holy Star, brother! Not here! You aren't bringing him here? He is unconsecrated!"

Kynan scarcely heard. *Who* was unconsecrated? And what did it matter? What did it matter now?

"Many things must change tonight, brothers," the Tactician said stonily. He strode to the door and swung it open.

Kynan raised his haunted eyes. There was a movement in the open archway.

The Tactician stepped forward holding the arm of a young man. To Kynan, it was the shock of looking into a mirror.

To Torquas the Poet, it was a supernatural horror that left him whimpering and pleading to be forgiven sins even he, in his endless inventiveness, could never have committed.

The twin sons of Torquas XII, Galacton, *the* Star King of the Galaxy, Hereditary Warleader of Vyka, and a dozen more resounding titles, had met at last.

Chapter Eighteen

How, then, may men rule themselves, Grand Master? The legends say there is the rule of none, the rule of one, the rule of some, and the rule of all. Autocracy is better than anarchy and nihilism. Oligarchy is better than dictatorship. But the best is democracy. However, do not ask me how democracy comes, brothers. I do not know.
—Emeric of Rhada, Grand Master of Navigators,
 The Dialogues, early Second Stellar Empire period

In line astern, the first elements of the advance squadron from Nyor approached the sanctuary. They came at low level, across the land and into the glare of the rising sun of Aurora.

And on the crest of the landward hills, another formation, Navigators carrying green fronds and leading a single mounted man, made a procession of somber black against the dun-colored flank of the Auroran land. Their chanting carried on the morning air. They moved slowly, as all religious processions do. At the head of the line four princes of the Order marched in the dust. Behind them rode a man on a war mare. He was dressed in homespun, but on his brow rested the circlet, jeweled with sunbursts, of *the* King.

Near the rear of the holy procession walked Janessa and Baltus, the warlock. They had been cowled and robed, and they went now under gentle guard, surrounded by chanting Navigators.

Janessa felt a strange premonition. The Navigators had appeared out of the early morning darkness, and they had taken her and Baltus to a place in the forest and draped them both in Navigator's robes. All of this had been done in silence, and no one would answer her questions. Where was Kynan? Whence came all these cowled men? And why did they walk in humble religious procession now toward that holy place her grandfather had ceded so long ago to the Order?

"Baltus," the girl said, "I'm frightened. Where is Kynan?"

The old warlock squeezed her arm and said nothing. Far ahead in the procession she could see Skua. And on her back was a man in homespun. He was far off and rode facing away from her. Kynan? But on his dark head rested the gemmed crown of the Galacton. She could see the morning light striking spears of brilliance from the jewels.

"Baltus—*what's happening?*"

"Look," the warlock said. He was watching the sky, and now she could see the five starships coming on slowly, the sunlight bright on the Imperial blazon on their prows.

Except for the chanting, there was no sound in the still morning. All around her, the priests walked with downcast eyes, their faces hidden by their cowls. She could smell the dusty warmth of their bodies and the bitter tang of their oiled mail. They were armored, but unarmed, and they held the green fronds with their folded arms across their chests.

Against the rising sun, the sanctuary was a jumble of walled towers, domes, and strangely formed antennas. The waters of the Great Inland Sea lay flat as a bowl of molten silver.

The girl raised her eyes to the sky to watch the majestic approach of the leading starship. In these surroundings, it was an awe-inspiring sight. The sunlight shimmered down the kilometer-long hull as it turned toward the center of the walled sanctuary. She could see the valve beginning to dilate, and within she could make out the ranks of armed men.

She looked again toward the enclave and noted the almost motionless figures of black-clad Navigators on the battlements. They seemed to be kneeling in prayer, although some of them stood at the bases of the strange metal projections extending above the ancient stone walls. It was difficult to be certain, but against the rising sun there seemed to be a wave-like distortion in the air around the sanctuary.

She touched Baltus on the sleeve and was about to ask him to explain what it was that she was seeing when the prow of the leading starship seemed to penetrate the peculiar radiance.

The great vessel was moving at a height of less than one hundred meters, and it was traveling slowly. But as the ship entered the distorted air, the bow dipped sharply toward the ground.

Janessa could see the momentary confusion in the open valve as the deck canted sharply under the gathered warmen's feet. It seemed to her that the starship checked, tried to reverse course. But the inertia of its great mass carried it forward, and in an instant it ceased to be a starship at all. The magical power that had held the ancient vessel from the earth of a thousand planets and had driven it at godlike speed between the stars seemed to die. The prow struck the hard soil outside the sanctuary battlements, crumpled as though it were paper. The long, graceful shape caved in, bulged, collapsed. Then the rest of the hull struck with a dull *crumping* sound. Tears appeared in the shining metal flanks. Explosions ripped pieces of metal high into the air. Men and pieces of men spun horribly against the sky. The spine of the vast ship broke. Shining metal girders appeared for an instant and then vanished in the rising cloud of dust and debris. She could hear, distantly, the rumble of fire and the screams of dying men. She turned, gasping, and buried her head in the warlock's chest, fighting not to be sick.

To Kynan the Navigator, sitting on Skua's broad back, wearing the circlet of power on his head and the false identity of his brother the Galacton, the crash of the great starship was like an awakening.

Since the confrontation with Torquas in the starship of the Five, he had been like a man in a dream. The ideals of a lifetime had been badly mauled by the discovery of the ruthlessness with which he had been used. Shocked, dismayed, overborne by the cold drive to power of the old princes of the Order, he had scarcely had time to consider the full implications of the scheme they referred to as "the *plan*."

To serve God and the Order had been his purpose in life. Now he found himself cast in the role of central figure in a monstrous impersonation, required to *become* Torquas—a Galacton forever in the debt and power of the Order. The boldness and cold calculation of the Five's *coup* was its strength. Given Torquas the Poet's weakness and his own inability to protest, the plan could change the course of history. The Order and the Empire, without the consent of the people —without even their knowledge—would become one power: implacable, indestructible, perhaps immortal.

It was these thoughts that filled the young Navigator's mind on the processional journey toward the sanctuary. But the sudden shocking death of the Vegan starship jolted Kynan more than even he could know. For the first time in memory, Navigators had killed Navigators. The crew of the starship, together with most of the troops on board, had died a sudden and violent death.

Kynan was shaken with an unfamiliar rage at the brutal pragmatism of the mighty. Where were the ideals of his beloved Order? Where were the lofty precepts he had been taught in the Theocracy?

On the plain before the sanctuary, the murdered starship burned. The remainder of the squadron, stunned by the swift destruction of the lead vessel, hovered uncertainly out of range of the meson screen.

The religious procession, too, had reached the plain, and the Tactician, with consummate showmanship, marshaled the cowled priest in a wide semicircle. Slowly, and with great solemnity, he led the false Galacton forward so that he could be seen by the shaken Navigators in the starships.

Kynan could feel the throbbing ache in his skull again, and he knew that the Technician was at his machines in the starship in the forest, urging him to take the homage of the stunned and confused men in the Vegan ships.

The brilliant sunlight bathed the plain. Kynan narrowed his eyes and looked at the flaming disk of Aurora: a star like thousands of other stars scattered across the swirling mass of the galaxy. *To rule, to be king of all—to accept the submission of all men, everywhere—* Could ever a man have been so tempted?

Skua whickered uneasily and pranced on the hard-packed soil of the plain. Kynan awoke from his reverie to see that the starships had landed, and a delegation of Navigators and Vegan officers were approaching the semicircle of priests.

He sat bareheaded in the morning, the sunlight flashing from the jeweled circlet on his brow. He seemed to be partaking of some strange and unbelievable dream. A voice whispered in his mind: *King—you are the Star King—these are your soldiers—your starships. The soil on which your charger stands is yours—the star that sheds its warmth on you is yours—* He felt the burning touch of a pride and arrogance that was like a consuming fire within him. *Why not?* Was his blood any different from the blood of him whose crown he wore? Wasn't he, too, descendant of a hundred generations of Vykan kings? What was the way of the Navigator compared to that?

He was not Kynan of Gonlan, Kynan the foundling, bondson to a petty chieftain, Kynan the Navigator. He was the Galacton, king of an empire of stars!

His eyes were no longer those of a simple pilot of starships. They were suddenly dark and farseeing, the eyes of a man with power—power greater than he had ever imagined one single human being could command.

The Vegan officers, astonished to see the Galacton here on Aurora, stood at rigid salute. The Navigators from the ships, still stunned by the seemingly supernatural force that had struck down the first vessel, were bareheaded before the frightening presence of the sovereign surrounded by priests and four princes of the Order.

The Logician was speaking. Kynan heard his words dimly, through the roaring pulse of his own blood in his ears.

"—the power of the holy Star has struck the forces of rebellion. Where is Tran? He must be brought to book for this!"

The Logician's voice was like the rumble of thunder to the Vegan warmen. They stood fearfully, waiting for the crushing word from the Galacton—this strangely possessed and burning king so terrifyingly different from the foppish dandy of Nyor.

Kynan heard himself speaking, and somewhere within him there was a tiny bead of despair, for in speaking now as Torquas, it seemed to him that he surrendered completely to the deception and all that it might entail for generations of men yet unborn.

The Vegans were accepting his orders unquestioningly, completely. This was the loyalty that Torquas, fool and dilettante, had never commanded. It had always been there, due to the blood of Glamiss the Magnificent and his descendants. It needed only to be demanded as the Galacton's due.

This, then, was the taste of power. Kynan, for the first time in his twenty years of life, sensed the true nature of his world. It was in the suddenly pleased fearfulness of the captains, in their willingness to respond to the leadership of blood, honor, and feudal privilege.

He touched Skua with his heels, and she stepped forward, out of the circle of priests and into the ranks of the warmen. Kynan addressed himself to a decorated regimental commander. "What is your name, warman?"

"Auden Veg Novens, King." The soldier's face, scarred with the marks of many battles, expressed the man's pride in being addressed directly by the Galacton.

Kynan heard a murmuring in the ranks of the Navigators behind him. He turned to look coldly at the Tactician. He felt a dour satisfaction. The princes had created a king, now let them accept him.

"You will take your regiment to Star Field, warman," Kynan said. "Starships of the Gonlani-Rhad will be arriving within the hour. You are to carry this message to First Minister LaRoss and General Crespus. Say to them that there is to be no fighting with the men of Star Field. Say that is by *my* command. Crespus and LaRoss are to come here—to me. Is that understood?"

"As you command, King." The Vegan gathered his staff and the Navigators of his ship and retreated across the plain.

Kynan looked achingly at the still smoldering ruins of the great ship that had crashed. Navigators from the sanctuary searched now in the rubble for survivors. It was a sight that filled Kynan with angry bitterness. He turned and searched the ranks of the cowled priests, searching for Janessa, but he could see nothing but the increasing alarm on the faces of the four members of the Five who had accompanied the procession from the starship in the forest.

He found a Vegan officer wearing the harness of a general officer and ordered him to disembark the troops in three of the grounded starships. "Deploy them for battle, warman," he said in a ringing voice.

This command brought forth a protest from the Tactician. Kynan looked down on him and said, "This is not a matter for priests, old man." His voice was flinty. "Or is there something you wish to say to the troops yourself, Navigator?"

The Tactician, with the look of a man who has created a monster, retreated and went into private conference with his three colleague princes. They would send word to the Technician now, Kynan knew, and the machines in the starship would begin to punish him for his insubordination. But he was a man adrift from his faith; he was beyond caring.

"Starships, King!" A Vegan officer pointed into the brightness of the rising sun. The second squadron of Imperial starships had arrived to attack the sanctuary.

Kynan gave an order to signal the leading ship. "General Veg Tran is to report to me. Personally and at once." He felt a sudden wry pleasure. How easily one became accustomed to the sense of power, he thought. How swiftly one learned to expect commands to be obeyed.

He watched the heliographed orders being flashed to the starships. To *his* starships. To the starships of the King.

"Set up a camp," he ordered, and then, with an almost hysterical pleasure, he added, "And keep these Navigators away from me. There has been too much interference by priests already!"

And he wondered: *How long now? How long before the Tactician and his machines began to fight him for possession of his own personality?* It was like waiting for a descent into hell.

Chapter Nineteen

Truth is found when men are free to pursue it.
  —Attributed to Franklin Delano Roosevelt,
    warleader of the American Millennium, middle
    Dawn Age. Fragment found at Tel-Manhat, Earth

*Let tomorrow take care of tomorrow— Leave future
things to fate.*
  —Attributed to Charles Swain, Dawn Age poet,
    period unknown. Fragment found at
    St. Francis Town, Earth

*For one strange moment in time, all power in the galaxy
was concentrated in the person of one unknown man
standing before a sanctuary on a hinterland planet of
the Rim. It was then that men learned the meaning of
the phrase: the way of the Navigator.*
  —Nav (Bishop) Julianus Mullerium,
    Anticlericalism in the Age of the Star Kings,
    middle Second Stellar Empire period

Kynan sat on a camp chair in the bannered pavilion set up for the Galacton's use by the staff of the Vegan regiments.

The sides of the tent flapped in the wind from the Inland Sea: their fluttering sound was the only thing heard within. Outside, the Vegs were drawn up in battle order, though their officers were uncertain whom they were expected to fight and when.

The Navigator searched the faces of the staff officers surrounding him. For the past twenty minutes he had been giving detailed instructions for the reception to be given General Alain Veg Tran and the men of the Gonlani-Rhad.

The Vegans were respectful and obedient. But Kynan could not help noticing the strangely puzzled expression that came across each man's face as he received orders from a king he had known before only as the Poet or the Fool.

"Among the Navigators who came with me from the hill, you will find the warlock Baltus and the heiress to this place, Janessa. I want them brought to me here. The prince Navigator who was with me will want to come as well—" He had to repress an ironic smile at that. The Tactician must be suffering badly now, thinking that he had forever shattered that holy *plan* that meant so much to him. "I will have him here, as well." He stood to indicate that the officers should be about their duties. "The First Minister of Gonlan and his general are to be put under guard as soon as they arrive. If the Royal Vulk of Rhada is with them, he is to come to me at once. General Veg Tran and all his officers will wait until I summon them. First, I will see all the Vykan regimental commanders here. See to it."

The Vegans saluted and withdrew. Kynan could hear them murmuring at the strangeness of the Galacton's behavior. But praetorians though they were—they would obey. With the power of the Galacton surrounding him, the Navigator never doubted it.

Presently, a Vegan officer appeared to report that the warlock and the Aurori girl were outside the tent.

"Send them to me. Alone," Kynan ordered.

"Alone, King?"

Kynan fixed the man with a hard look. "Warman, understand this—and make certain that all officers of the army understand it as well. When your ruler gives an order, it is to be obeyed. At once and without question. The time of the light shows is over."

The officer's eyes widened with surprise, and he saluted formally. "Yes, Warleader. Certainly."

"Send the girl and the warlock to me."

Baltus and Janessa, still wearing the cowled clericals of Navigators, entered the tent. Kynan received them with a sad half-smile on his face. The girl's face went pale at the sight of him.

"*Kynan*—it *is* you!" she exclaimed.

Baltus touched her lips with his fingertips and shook his head. "Be careful what you say," he murmured. "The Vegans are only just outside the tent."

Kynan took the older man by the hand and drew him into the center of the pavilion. "You don't seem surprised, Baltus," he said.

"I suspected," the warlock said. "Your bond-father knew who you were—and though he never told me, I suspected that this might be true. You are brothers, you and Torquas. By the Star, who could tell you apart?"

"You could," Kynan said. And looking gently at Janessa, he added, "And you, Princess?"

The girl's eyes were fixed on the Galacton's circlet of power on Kynan's brow. Her expression was a mixture of relief, perplexity, and a growing anxiety. "If you are Kynan, then where is—*he?*" She could not bring herself to pronounce the Galacton's name.

Baltus regarded the Navigator speculatively. "Now what will you do, Kynan?" He knew what temptation was. He understood what the Navigator was facing.

Kynan drew his Navigator's pistol from his harness and handed it to Baltus. "Do you know how this weapon works?"

The warlock smiled thinly. "At the risk of profaning one of your precious mysteries—yes, I do."

"Torquas may have been taken back to the starship in the forest," Kynan said.

"Yes, I think so. A party of Navigators went back the way we had come as soon as you joined the Vegan officers."

Kynan shuddered. Soon the power of the Technician's machines would begin to attack his brain in an attempt to force him back into the pattern of the Five's plan to take power for the Order. There was little time left, and there was still so much to do...

"I want you to take Skua and ride back to the starship. Give the Navigators there this message: They are to send Torquas to me with you. They are to do it at once and without question—or I shall lead the Vegans and the Vyk regiments into the sanctuary and take *for the Empire* what they make there."

"You will burn, apostate—" The Tactician stood at the tent entrance, his face livid with anger.

Janessa drew closer to Kynan, and even the warlock was shaken by the prince Navigator's words.

Only Kynan remained unmoved. To Baltus, he said, "Go and do as I tell you. Time is very short."

Baltus shoved past the Tactician and departed.

An officer entered, saluted, and said, "King, the Vykan regimental commanders are waiting for you."

"In a moment," Kynan said.

The Tactician swept into the tent and, ignoring the girl, said bitterly, "You are a Navigator, a priest of God and a servant of the Order. If you do not obey me, what I said will come to pass. There will be a burning for the first time in a hundred years!"

Kynan pressed his fingertips to his temples and said, in a voice of cold hatred, "Not even the love I bear the Order can justify what you have done to me. And the holy Star knows that you have done it badly—"

"The Vulk interfered with your conditioning. But for that, there would have been no problems. You would never have needed to know."

Kynan marveled at the cynicism of the worldly priest. "And the Empire would have been ruled by the Order—through *me*—"

The old priest's eyes narrowed. "Would that be so bad a thing? Have you no loyalty to the Order which has guided you, cared for you, taught you?"

"I have a loyalty, priest," Kynan said scornfully. "But not

one that you and your colleagues would understand."

The Tactician seemed to notice Janessa for the first time. His voice was steely. "This girl will have to be conditioned. She can't be allowed to remember what she is hearing here."

Kynan said, "Janessa won't be touched. Not by you. Not by anyone. I say it."

"*You* say it?" The prince Navigator gave a barking laugh. "Do you think you are a *real* king, then?"

Kynan's teeth bared in a grim smile. "I am what you have made me, Father."

The Tactician threw up his hands. "We've made you mad. We—the Vulk—all of us. We've driven you insane."

"Perhaps you have. But it's a useful madness, Father. Now let me tell you what you are going to do."

"*You* are giving orders to *me?*"

Kynan nodded grimly. "And you are going to obey them. Let me tell you why."

"Oh, yes. Do that, little priest."

"*Not* little priest, father. Galacton. King. Commander of the Starfleets."

"Madness!"

"Hear me."

The Tactician subsided into uneasy silence.

"What does the Grand Master know of your precious plan? Very little, I'll venture to guess. Perhaps nothing at all. Like so many power-elites in our history, you and your friends have decided *you* know what is best for the Order, for the Empire. Am I right?" The Tactician did not reply, and Kynan went on, with growing savagery and anger. "Do you know what would happen if I were to step outside this moment and tell the army what you have done?"

Alarm leapt into the old priest's eyes. "They would tear you to pieces," he exclaimed.

"Probably. But they would destroy the Order, too. They would storm every sanctuary, murder every priest-Navigator, take over the starships themselves— And what if they knew that there is a nuclear weapon on board your starship? And that others are probably being constructed in this very sanctuary, now, at this moment?"

"You really are insane," the Tactician said hoarsely.

"Would you bring the Dark Time again?"

Kynan's eyes were cold. "Then do we understand one another?"

"But you *couldn't*," the old priest said. "You are a *Navigator*."

"I am also a man—a man who has been tampered with, pushed, driven, and stripped of everything I was taught to live by."

"Your bond-father was proud of his part in the plan," the Tactician said desperately. "He was a religious man, he knew—"

Kynan cut him off with a gesture. "Kreon was my bond-father. My *father* was Torquas, *the* Star King. Do you deny that?"

"Of course I don't deny that. Yours is the blood of Glamiss—"

Kynan's smile was not pleasant. "Then I am King."

The Tactician rubbed his beard. His eyes had suddenly become haunted. "You were the second son. I was there. I saw it—"

"Prove it, priest," Kynan said icily.

The Tactician shook his head slowly. "I—cannot."

"Then I am King," Kynan said again.

"You—are—King."

"Better," Kynan said.

"What will you do?" the old man asked slowly.

"First I will tell you what *you* will do."

The prince Navigator nodded painfully.

"You will send orders to the sanctuary that all production of energy weapons will stop *at once*. We have no need for such things. Those weapons already assembled will be dismantled."

"You cannot wipe out knowledge," the Navigator said pleadingly.

Kynan gave a harsh laugh. "No, I cannot. But isn't that what the Order has been doing for the last two hundred years? Slowing discoveries, guarding dangerous scientific developments? If I am wrong, then the Order is wrong. If I am right, then the Order has meaning—in spite of men like you and your planners. I cannot stop Navigators from thinking about weapons—but I *can* stop them from building them. For now, for this time, that is all one man can do. But it *shall be* as I say, priest."

The Tactician understood power, even in the hands of another. "It shall be done," he said, low.

Kynan touched his temples again with fingers trembling with anger and loathing. "This thing you did to me. Can it be undone?"

"No. It cannot."

"Very well. If the machines attempt once more to control me, I may not be able to stand it. I have given orders to the Vegans that if I am taken with a sickness of the mind, they are to hold you responsible and attack the sanctuaries."

Fear flared into the Tactician's eyes.

Kynan regarded him bitterly. "I see that you have ordered the Technician to try the machines once more."

The man's fear was answer enough.

"Then you had better send word."

"And if I do all these things?" The old priest had courage enough to bargain, even now.

"The Order will be safe."

"And you will be King," the old Navigator said in a dead voice.

"That need no longer concern you," Kynan said in a tone of dismissal.

The sun stood high in the pale Auroran sky as the Galacton stepped out of his tent to review the assembled Imperial power.

As Imperial armies went in that time, the force was formidable. The Vegan division, less only those men who had died in the crash of the starship, was drawn up on the seaward flank of the sanctuary. The thirty Vyk regiments, the personal troops of the Vykan Galactons, formed an assault force commanding the landward approaches to the plain.

The Vegan horses glittered in the sunlight, their scaly carapaces silvery under the massed lances and banners of the heavy cavalry corps. The Vykan regiments stood dismounted, their Rhadan mounts murmuring to one another in ragged ranks behind the armed men.

On the walls of the sanctuary, black-clad Navigators surveyed the Imperial force uneasily. From within the complex of laboratories and monastery buildings, they could hear the scurry of activity as the scientist-Navigators, furiously complaining but disciplined, went about the business of dismantling a number of devices, the purpose of which the junior Navigators on the walls could only guess.

A delegation of Navigators had entered the enclave less than an hour before, led by a prince of the Order. Now the junior priests and novices on the battlements stood to their weapons and regarded the massed Imperial forces on the plain, wondering if they would soon face an attack.

The meson screen that had brought the starship down still shimmered in the morning air; but it was a useless defense against an old-style assault by armed men.

To the east, the Great Inland Sea lay placid and blue to the horizon. No movement of any kind stirred the surface of the water. The sunlight reflected from the mirror surface, and it seemed that all the massed men and the priests on the sanctuary walls waited for the decision of the King.

Kynan, alone now, walked slowly through the ranks of fighting men to the hollow square of the staff, where the legendary General Veg Tran and the leaders of the Gonlani invasion force waited under discreet Vykan guard.

Though Kynan had never seen Tran, he recognized him instantly. The man's bearing and honors made him unmistakable. Tran, on the other hand, thinking that he had a poet suddenly gone mad to deal with, waited, furiously impatient, amid his officers.

His mind was a seething mass of angry thoughts. The Navigators—always the *priests*. They had dared to bring the foolish Torquas to this place, dared to check momentarily the great scheme he, the Empire's greatest general, had set into motion. By the Star, someone would pay for this—!

He saw the Galacton approaching and felt a thrill of uncertainty. It was Torquas, surely. But a Torquas unlike the foolish, hemp-smoking King he had left in Nyor.

There was a strength in the young face that he had never seen before, a sense of purpose in the blue Vykan eyes. Tran's confidence faltered infinitesimally. But no, it would take more than a cutting of hair and a clean-shaven face, more than a voyage with the Navigators, to make Torquas the Fool into a real king. Tran knew where the real power resided: in the troops, in the army—and soon, in the AbasNavs and in himself.

He drew himself up and spoke to his sovereign. "I thought I had left you safe in Nyor, King."

The reply was stunning, cold and unyielding as a sword blade on flesh. *"I thought I had a loyal general. We were both wrong, Alain Veg Tran."*

Tran's face suffused with the blood of sudden fury. *Torquas the Fool—speaking like this—to me,* he thought, raging.

He laid his hand on his sword hilt in an instinctive gesture, and the Vykans gave an angry growl, the ranks moving forward. The Galacton stopped them with a gesture. He spoke to Tran in clear, deliberate tones. "You came on the pretense of keeping the peace among the Gonlani-Rhad and the Aurori. Yet you sent my troops *here*. Now a starship has been lost and my soldiers with it." Kynan fixed the general with a cold, angry stare. He was feeling the intoxication of power and the anger that only great power could indulge. *"I know why you came, Tran.* But the Star King is father to his people. I arrived before you. What you seek is being destroyed at this very moment—"

General Veg Tran felt his great design crumbling around him. To be defeated was bad enough. But to be frustrated by one he had thought a weakling and a fool was almost more than the proud Vegan could bear.

The Galacton spoke more to the army than to him. "This is my judgment, Alain Veg Tran. In recognition of your services to the Empire in the past, you will retain your rank. But in punishment for treachery, treason, and high crimes against the Empire, you are banished to your estates in Vega. There you will spend the rest of your days under Vykan guard without the power to command any but your personal servants—"

Tran's fury seemed to choke him. *This fool, this drug-addled fop—was acting the great King—banishing Tran, the victor of Eridanus—the unquestioned leader of the AbasNavs —the army—*

A cry, rage-driven, burst from him. *"Vegans! To me! I am your general—!"*

The Vegan troops stood unmoving, humiliation on the faces of their officers. Auden Veg Novens, the Vegan officer who had brought Crespus and LaRoss in arrest to this place before the sanctuary, could bear the disgrace no more. He stepped forward and struck Veg Tran across the face. "You are addressing the *King,* warman!"

"The King!" cried a derisive voice. *"The great Star King!"*

Kynan saw the ranks of Tran's officers part and a familiar figure step forward, arrogant and proud.

It was Karston.

He pointed a finger at Kynan and shouted to the warmen. "Is *that* your Galacton? Your King of the Universe?"

Kynan felt a sick despair. It was done, over. He had risked everything on one bold stroke, and out of nowhere Karston had appeared to strip the royal robes from him and expose him naked before the nobles.

"Let *me* tell you about this dazzling king of yours—"

The words were blotted out by a sharp explosion. Karston's face crinkled into an expression of startled amazement. He pressed his hand to his mailed chest and blood flowed, bright red in the sunshine, between his fingers.

Kynan, too surprised to move, watched his bond-brother sink first to his knees, then, slowly, onto his face in the sandy ground. He turned to see behind him the Tactician, a smoking flintlock pistol in his hand.

The prince Navigator let fall the weapon and made the sign of the Star. "Blasphemy," he said to the stunned assemblage. "He spoke blasphemy against the anointed King." His old eyes sought Kynan's, and the young Navigator saw there the worldly priest's unspoken plea to understand that what he had done was a thing that must be.

Kynan understood the dreadful ache, the price of power. Understanding, he was sickened.

He raised his eyes to the sanctuary, remembering the stillness of the cloisters, the sense of purpose and goodness that he had once felt in his call to the way of the Navigator.

That was all done now. The Order would go on, of course, but the way was no longer open—not for him. *A priest of God must be innocent,* he thought. *To serve the Star, a man must be sure of goodness.* And he knew with deep sadness that he could never be so sure again.

He stepped forward and knelt at Karston's side. Gently, he rolled the dead man over and drew the sign of the Star on his forehead. The silent soldiers watched, wondering. But Kynan was studying the dead face and remembering his childhood on the sea cliffs of Melissande. *We did not love one another, Karston,* he thought, *but we were brothers—*

And then it came to him that he had, in truth, a brother—that another shared with him the blood of the Vykan herdsman kings.

He stood and said to the Tactician, "Is all done in the sanctuary?"

"Yes, King." The old priest seemed almost spent now, done with a lifetime of plotting and politics. And what had it come to? A dead starship, dead men, and a false King—

"I think it best that all leave this place now," Kynan said.

"Let it be so," the Tactician said, defeated.

In the stillness of the tent, Kynan could hear the sounds of the army quietly embarking. There was still a smell of death in the air from the wreckage of the shattered starship. It was a bitter tang, redolent of the centuries the mighty vessel had served men and of its shameful death.

Kynan said to Baltus, "Leave us. I would speak to my brother."

The warlock, sensing Kynan's sadness, departed silently.

Kynan approached the hunched figure in homespun cowl and plain soldier's mail. "Torquas," he said.

The Galacton stirred but did not speak. He seemed still crushed by the tumultuous mishaps of the last days.

"Torquas," Kynan said again. "Hear me."

The twin face, that mirror image of his own, turned toward him. "I hear you," the boy murmured.

Kynan wondered: *We are exactly of an age—why do I feel so much older?* He said, "Do you know what has happened?"

"I saw it all. The priest killed your bond-brother."

"Yes."

"Because he was going to tell the army that there are two of us. The priests will kill anyone who does that." There was genuine fear in his voice.

Kynan took the jeweled circlet from his head and held it, looking at the play of light on the gems and metal. With this went the power to rule men wherever they were found in the galaxy— Then he thought: *No, that isn't right.* The crown was but the outward symbol of the authority men gave willingly to their King. Without that willingness, there was no power. And one day men would cease to bestow it. They would rule themselves.

"Can that be so?" Torquas asked, and Kynan realized that he must have spoken aloud.

"Not in our time, perhaps, brother. But one day," he said.

"I wish it were so now," Torquas said with sudden feeling. "It's too great a burden for one man."

Kynan smiled slowly and sadly. "I've found it so."

"And so have I!" Torquas exclaimed. "All I ever wanted was to be a poet—Kynan." He pronounced his brother's strange Rhadan name for the first time and smile tentatively. Then he looked at the circlet in Kynan's hands and shuddered. "Must I die too? To keep our secret?"

Kynan placed the crown on his brother's head. "You are firstborn," he said formally. "You are the King."

Torquas touched the metal unbelievingly, his eyes fixed on Kynan's somber face. Within him a maelstrom of emotions whirled. For a time, despite his fear, he had been free. Now he was free no longer. He was human enough to voice a protest, but Kynan stopped him.

"You are firstborn," he said again. "You were trained to be a King; I to be a Navigator. Now you must be a better King, and I can no longer be a Navigator."

"But the priests chose *you.*"

"The ambitious priests in the Order would have liked to rule the Empire through me, brother. But that can't be. It is a step backward, toward the Dark Time. Power must be dispersed— not concentrated. That is the trend of history. You are the King."

With these words, Kynan raised his brother to his feet, and then, in a gesture as old as all the empires of men, he knelt before his sovereign.

Perhaps, he thought, he imagined it. But it seemed that Torquas stood straighter and more proudly. With a touch of self-mocking irony, he thought, too: *He is not a good King, but he is the true King. That much I can do for the spirit of the Star that was taught me by the Order.*

Torquas pulled him to his feet and embraced him. It was a very non-Gonlani gesture, this display of affection between men. It was the way of a Vykan. *And I am no Vykan,* Kynan thought suddenly. *My world is here, on the Rim.*

"Confirm me in my bond-father's kingship, Torquas. That is all I ask. If I can no longer be a Navigator, let me at least be a Rhad again."

Torquas spoke wonderingly, "No more than that?"

"Yes. This much more. *Be* Galacton, brother. Rule well. And," Kynan added more gently, "remember that you have a brother who calls you King."

They stood now for a moment in the entrance to the tent with the high sun of Aurora on them, Torquas crowned, Kynan cowled as a priest for what he knew would be the last time. Far off, near the last of the starships remaining before the sanctuary, the Vykan officers awaited their warleader.

"Baltus," Kynan spoke to the warlock quietly. "Take the King to his officers."

Torquas embraced Kynan once more and asked, "Will we meet again, brother?"

Kynan smiled ruefully. "That wouldn't be wise, would it."

The Galacton protested.

Kynan shook his head. "The Empire isn't ready for *two* kings, Torquas."

Kynan watched the warlock and the Vykan depart. *Will I ever regret what I gave up,* he wondered? The Star knew how tempted he had been. But no, the probes in his brain were there for all time. He could make them harmless only by making himself harmless—as a petty kinglet, one among thousands.

He saw Janessa coming across the plain, and his sadness lifted. There were worse things than to be warleader and king of the Gonlani-Rhad. With Janessa beside him, he would not dream those wonderful-fearful dreams of a galaxy, a river of stars in his hands.

Skua appeared and nipped at him with her blunted old teeth. "Ky-nan again," she said. He looked into the slotted eyes with interest. There was wisdom everywhere. One only had to search for it.

"Home," the mare said.

"Yes, home now," he replied. His lips firmed into a hard, straight line of determination. There was still LaRoss to be dealt with. It would be a harsh judgment, given in the manner of a Rim star king.

And Triad with the Royal Vulk to come. Yes, Gret had promised. He could relive adventures from the Age of Heroes. What did giving up an empire compare to that?

Janessa had paused to watch the last Imperial starship lifting. A breeze had risen and was blowing fresh from the Inland Sea.

Kynan raised his hand and waved to her. She turned and ran toward him. He thought about Evart and Pius and Clement waiting with his ship in the forest—waiting to make the last journey he would ever make as a consecrated Navigator. If there was a sadness there, it was lessened by his certainty that they, and thousands of others like them, would roam the galaxy for centuries yet to come, bringing the peace of God to generations of men yet unborn. And the Order—the dedicated priests who were the *real* Order—would never know what he had done to keep it pure. What did it matter?

He thought of a line of poetry written by a long-dead man of Earth's Dawn Age. It was as true now as it had been when it was written: "Let tomorrow take care of tomorrow— Leave future things to fate."

Thinking that, he stepped forward to take Janessa in his arms.